Just One Weekend

Catherine Aitken

To Lynn
I hope you enjoy
the book.
Catherine x

Handbag Press

ISBN 978-1-7394756-2-8

Handbag Press 2024

BY THE SAME AUTHOR

The Liberation of Bella McCaa

ABOUT THE AUTHOR

Catherine always wanted to be a writer and couldn't believe her luck when her first job was as office junior for Jackie Magazine. But wanderlust took her travelling until she segued into a career in the film and TV industry, eventually working in script development and producing drama. To supplement the lean years in film development, Catherine created an accessories brand that she ran in tandem with feature film pursuits. Now she is concentrating on her own stories and her debut novel, *The Liberation of Bella McCaa*, was published in 2023. It is now joined by *Just One Weekend*. Catherine hails from Dundee but lives in Leith, Edinburgh and is currently writing her third book.

Find out more at www.catherineaitken.com

To my sisters, Maggie and Janet, who are always there.

CHAPTER 1

Music blasted out of the speaker and Sandy could resist no longer. Flinging the dust buster on the sofa, she danced around the living room as one of her favourite tracks from The Brig beat a rhythm through her body. She could not wait to fly off to New York and see them live. She pounded the air with imaginary sticks, keeping perfect time with the drum intro. Then the melodic pop rock of the band swelled and the singer's voice came in with the loud 'Hey, Hey, Hey' of "Boys from Nowhere". She raised both arms to the ceiling, turning full circle as she let herself go. Her bare feet slid across the carpet as a vigorous drum solo reached a crescendo, and she pummelled the cushions in time to the beat. For the finale, she danced around the armchairs playing an imaginary sax with the brass section, then roared out the lyrics of the last verse, eyes closed, arms high and swaying – until a loud knock broke into her trance. There was her neighbour standing in front of the bay window grinning and giving her a handclap. Sandy waved uncertainly as the neighbour retreated.

Embarrassed, she moved away and caught a glimpse of herself in the mirror. Her hair had come loose from its tight clasp and she tucked it into place, dampening her fingers to force obstinate strands to behave. Reducing the volume of the next track from her phone, she resumed hoovering invisible dust particles from the bookcase, ensuring the row of travel guides created a precise line on the shelf. She inspected the room and, satisfied all was in order, she plucked five copies of laminated A5 sheets from the table and checked them.

NEW YORK WEEKEND

THURSDAY 18th April

01.30 Meet Airport Café (02.00 for Is.)***

05.05 Flight Edinburgh to Newark

08.15 Arrive Newark Airport

08.45 AirTrain to Penn St. (40 mins)

09.25 Walk from Penn St. to City Hotel (20 mins)

09.45 Arrive City Hotel East 34th & Lexington (Receipt on Google Docs)

09.45-10.10 Shower and unpack. Walk 20 mins to:

10.30 Brunch at Tick Tock Diner (481 8th Ave/34th Booked)

11.30 Allow 90 mins for walk and subway to:

13.00 Liberty & Ellis Island Ferry (Tix on phone)

16.00 Return Battery Park for City Bike tour (App downloaded)**

18.00 Grand Central Station Walking Tour (Booked)

19.30 Dinner at Grand Central Oyster Bar (Booked)

22.00 Return to hotel

The tiny print of the details continued in the same vein on both sides until their return flight on the Monday. Mobile in hand, Sandy entered the kitchen and stuck one of the laminated sheets to the fridge with a magnet of the Guggenheim Bilbao. The music was playing in the kitchen, too, coming from a speaker set high on the wall, and her head bobbed in time as she opened the freezer and examined the evenly stacked containers, labelled with their contents. Removing a couple, she rejigged the stacks and placed the selected ones inside the fridge for defrosting. Satisfied, she rearranged a tea towel that was hanging on the cooker and adjusted the cutlery and condiments at the single-place setting on the table.

In the bedroom she drew a neatly manicured thumb over a list of tracks on her mobile entitled "The Brig – My Faves" and selected "Goodbye" – an anthemic ballad she loved about leaving people and places, a stripped-down version of single vocal and guitar. She sang as she removed her suit from where it hung on the door and inspected it for creases. Her attention moved to a carry-on case where her clothes were packed, each item wrapped in tissue. Liquids and potions for the trip had been decanted into marked bottles and fitted into the polythene security container she tucked into her shoulder bag. Taking out a small notebook, she ticked off the last items on a long to-do list.

In the bathroom, she showered and washed her hair, taking time to dry it as straight as possible and then wound her golden locks away in a tight knot. Dressed in the smart beige suit and a pair of sensible walking shoes, she left a schedule on one of the pillows of the double bed and went downstairs with her luggage.

She opened a cupboard in the living room and pulled out a well worn cardboard box. She flipped the lid off and raked amongst the Brig ticket stubs from the 90s and the 00s, a stack of the band's CDs, and some fan magazines. Other memorabilia included an ancient jotter with four angelic-looking young men on the front – this was ornately hand-decorated with the name of the lead guitarist and a heart with an arrow through it pointing at his head. She smiled at the sight and rummaging further found photographs of her teenage self with her friend, Isobel, photo-booth relics where they posed and preened for the camera in dubious fashions, clothing long gone and rightly forgotten. She took out her mobile and captured the photos of their past. She lingered over the souvenirs she'd collected, bought with much hilarity and joy in a different time, and stored away for years: keyrings, notebooks and even a small mirror with the face of the lead guitarist.

Hours later Sandy stared out at the night from the living room window. For a moment her own image became the focus and she was caught unawares by the vision of her middle-aged self. She tried to find something of that young woman from the past in the reflection. Her curls were under control but dark circles, pronounced by the dim lighting, were evident beneath her eyes and her expression was serious. It was so different from the happy and hopeful teenagers they'd been, blissfully unaware of the curveballs life could throw at them. Headlights erased the reflection as a car turned into the drive, and her husband, Mike, appeared.

'Sorry I'm so late, love. We got that crane on site – not as tall as Big Carl – remember I told you about that one? Still huge though! Tricky machine to work with.' He removed his high-vis jacket as Sandy presented her cheek to be kissed.

'It's nearly eleven, Mike – crazy hours. There's lasagne if you're still hungry?'

'Not sure, might be a bit late to eat now.'

'You need fuel working so late. There's two meals defrosting for tomorrow and more in the freezer. There's a schedule on the fridge and in the bedroom with a copy to Google Docs. My taxi should be here soon—'

Mike's mobile rang and scooping it out of his shirt pocket, he held a finger in the air for quiet while he answered. 'Hi. Not a problem... Yes, of course...' Sandy watched her husband as he talked to his colleague, then he ended the call and said, 'They want me in London early Saturday for a meeting with the big honchos.'

'That's mad. You need time off to rest. And we can't make plans while you're like this—'

'This is the last job, Sandy, I promise. Think of me working hard while you and Isobel are swanning around the Big Apple. I'm so jealous.'

Sandy frowned. 'I did ask you before I spoke to Isobel; you could've been coming with me.'

'I know, I know, but I can't let them down. And you'll have a much better time reliving your teenage fantasies with Isobel than with me.' He smiled as he collapsed on an easy chair. 'Anyhoo, it's only 'til the end of this contract. Scout's honour, and then we can do as much travelling you like.' He held up three fingers in a childish salute.

'You said that last time. And what'll we do about New York?' Sandy could see her husband drifting off into work mode again.

'I can't believe we got the crane, it's the biggest one I've had on site.' Mike leaned a hand over the back of the chair towards her. 'Sorry. Did you say something about New York?'

'It's on your bucket list too. Never mind. Here's the taxi.' Sandy retrieved her luggage.

Mike gave her a hug. 'I am sorry you know, but work...'

'I'm sorry too, for nagging. I just want us to go away on a long trip, have an adventure.'

'We will. When you get home we'll get the books out, chart a route, start booking. OK? You'll have the best time with Isobel.' He kissed Sandy's proffered cheek as she moved towards the door. 'Love you.'

'Love you too.'

On the street, she wheeled her case towards the taxi.

'What time's your flight?' the driver asked.

'5.05 am to New York.'

'Jings lassie, it's Edinburgh Airport you're going to, not Heathrow. I'll take the Perth Road.'

'Go via the B road, it cuts about seven minutes off before we get to the dual carriageway.'

'We've got plenty of time.'

'I want to stick to my timetable. There might be an accident or a tyre blowout or something.' Sandy strapped the seat belt on and the driver took his place behind the wheel.

'Life is what happens to you when you're making plans,' he said. 'John Lennon said that.'

'No he didn't,' she retorted. 'He said life is what happens to you when you're busy making *other* plans. That's completely different.'

She chose to ignore the driver rolling his eyes as he pulled away and they were soon out of the housing estate, leaving Dundee far behind.

CHAPTER 2

Jake lay flat out on the king-sized bed and puffed out a long sigh. He eyed his protruding belly sticking out from the frilly white shirt he was half wearing, a single button straining the threads and ready to pop any minute. He had one leg in a pair of jeans, stuck at the knee. The bedroom was strewn with clothes, trousers hanging off the wardrobe door, a shirt hooked onto a painting. An open suitcase lay in the middle of the room, empty save for a well-worn sweatshirt. Outside a car honked.

'I'm coming!' he shouted. 'Can you not give a man peace!' He shook out tablets from a bottle and crunched them loudly. Lifting a pair of hefty weights from the floor, he pumped them as he walked around the chaotic room in his boxers, dragging the jeans around on one leg.

With a last 'Arrgh,' he lifted the weights above his head and let go. They fell with a dull, heavy thud. He tugged the jeans off and pitched them at the window. His frilly shirt followed, a button ripped off in the process. Two strides took him to a large walnut dresser, and opening the top drawer he removed small piles of boxers and socks and threw them into the case. Another drawer was opened revealing T-shirts, and he tried them on one by one. Those he managed to get on were flung on top of the underwear, those he couldn't were crushed into a ball and fired into the waste basket. Why had he gotten so fat? He chose the final T-shirt to wear, and grabbing a kilt from the floor he pulled it around his waist, utilising the ingeniously designed string extensions to secure the sides in place. Why, oh why had he agreed to this weekend?

He gathered a bunch of guitar picks and string packs from the bed and placed them in a small equipment box. That and a variety of cables and headphones followed the clothing. He marched into the bathroom and soon returned with toothbrush, toothpaste and a can of deodorant and pitched them in from the door. Fumbling behind a stack of books, he dug out an Aran jumper and pushed his head through, lifting his beard out and flattening it over his chest. Leather jacket and boots completed the outfit.

Grabbing a battered canvas bag from the floor, he placed a small laptop, notebook, and pens inside. He organised paper sheets of differing shapes and sizes lying across the duvet, into a tidy pile. The pages were covered in tight script, interspersed with musical notes and drawings, and he carefully laid them in a tattered leather document folder, held together with Sellotape yellowed with age. Adding the folder to his bag, he wore it across his body and pushing his hands into his hair, mangled the shapeless tangle into a man-bun with the help of a floral scrunchy. He shut the suitcase and jerked it upright.

Wheeling his belongings behind him, he went out into a cramped hallway, his head almost touching the ceiling. At the front door he stopped and opening a metal cupboard on the wall full of flashing lights and tiny screens, he input a long code, instantly setting off a series of high-pitched beeps. Reaching for a guitar case waiting at the door, he stepped outside, closed the door behind him and placed keys in various locks, listening as the tumblers fell into place. The beeping stopped.

'Let me put these in the boot for you, mate.' The taxi driver organised the luggage and got in the car.

Jake paused, hand on the passenger door handle, pulling at his beard as he peered at the surrounding emptiness of the late-night countryside. He inhaled deeply, then opened the car door and took a seat in the back. He fixed his gaze forward as the driver negotiated a bumpy track, onto a B road and drove into the night.

CHAPTER 3

Sandy waved as she saw Isobel running towards the café, a huge travel bag bouncing behind her. 'Did you bring the kitchen sink?'

Isobel sank into the seat opposite and snorted. 'Ha bloomin' ha. No. Jodie wanted the carry-on to take to Granny's. Anything for a quiet life.' Her response had been almost drowned out by an excruciating rendition of "Cheeky Baby" coming from close quarters. A group of excitable young women had squashed themselves into a booth and were belting the ubiquitous pop tune out. Paper hats on heads and printed tops heralded they were off to celebrate Ashley's Hen Weekend. Isobel sang with them while Sandy plugged her ears.

'I hate that song! Let's go and check in. Breakfast on the other side?'

'Good idea.'

They headed off to the check-in desks, the second verse of "Cheeky Baby" ringing in their ears. Joining the queue, Sandy took out the schedules and handed one to Isobel. 'Here you go.'

'Is this actually laminated?' Isobel teased, waving it in the air between thumb and forefinger.

'Hey! It makes sense to laminate it, stops it from being dirty and crumpled, and you can clearly see where you're meant to be at any given time. It'll fit in your bag.'

Isobel examined the list. 'You've even allowed for my lateness!'

'I like to be prepared.'

'I can't believe we're going to see The Brig! It's been forever.'

'Saturday night 8 pm. Standing room only. Better view, better atmosphere as well, don't you think?'

'Yes! I'll be drooling over Iain McDonald, same as I ever did. He is still so gorge – must be the clean living he's supposed to be into these days. It's going to be fantastic!'

'I know! I'm so glad Mike wasn't up for it—'

'Hold on a minute! You asked Mike before you asked me?'

'I had to. It's our anniversary, but I knew he wouldn't take leave from work. Anyway, it'll be much more fun if we can drool over them together, even though they're ancient now, too. I wonder if Jake Cabrelli is still good looking after all these years? I meant to look but forgot.'

'He was such a cutie pie. You had those posters on your wall for yonks!'

'I was gutted that Mum threw them away when I got married.' Sandy smiled at the memory. 'Do you think he'll have aged well?'

'Stop it! You've got the same dewy eyes you used to have when we went to see them. You're a grown woman of forty-seven!'

'He'll be fifty, so it's fine. I'm not leching after a young man.'

'You are in your head.'

'True!' They chuckled together as they inched forward to the check-in desk.

'Speaking of tall skinny men, Mike's stayed the same, hasn't he? Slightly less hair, that's it.'

'I wish he'd hand in his notice. I'm fed up waiting for him.'

Isobel wasn't paying attention. 'I'm sure Brian and I would have been like you and Mike, still loved up after twenty years.'

Sandy shrugged. 'Maybe. It's not perfect though.'

'Solid. You're solid, after everything you've been through together. I wonder what Brian would have been like? A roly-poly like me probably. He was always fond of his grub.'

'You are not a roly-poly – you've got a great figure – and a bust.' Sandy regarded her friend. 'You've done so well. That was the right move, wasn't it, to be nearer Brian's mum and dad?'

'They've been a godsend although he's still the person I want to tell when things happen with the kids. But I'm into my dating, despite the bloody frogs. I like Chip. A lot. Shame he's in Texas!' Isobel pouted like a baby. 'Virtual dates are not the same—'

'Next!' called the man at the check-in desk.

Sandy moved off but Isobel dropped her backpack and the contents fell out. She bent to help. 'Go ahead, Sands, I'm fine.' Isobel scooped the contents and tried to get organised as Sandy moved forward to the desk, paper-work and passport at the ready. She hoped she appeared a confident and experienced international traveller in her elegant suit, although she didn't feel it.

The attendant examined her passport and then Sandy, scrutinising the smart woman in front of him. 'We have a problem with a double booking in economy for this trip and we're offering a free upgrade to first class. Would you be interested in moving?'

'I'm travelling with—' Sandy started.

'You would be totally helping us out if you could.'

'Yes, she would be interested,' said Isobel, who was now standing behind her. 'Go on, Sandy.'

'We're travelling together, can't we both—'

'There's only space for one, sorry. Never mind.'

'No.' Isobel raised a hand. 'Wait a minute. Sandy – think about this – why should both of us be squashed into economy if you have the chance to travel in style. First class!'

'It doesn't seem right.'

'It does seem right and I absolutely don't mind.'

'Are you sure?'

'Yes! We're only going to sleep anyway.' Isobel smiled at the young man at the desk. 'She'll be ecstatically happy to take the offer, thank you.'

Sandy's new ticket and seat details were printed out. 'Have a good flight. Don't forget, you can use the premier lounge where there's a free breakfast.' The attendant glanced at Isobel. 'Only for premier passengers of course.'

'Of course!' Isobel murmured as she was checked in and moved off. 'I'll bet yours is the last one. If it takes wearing a suit to get bumped up, I'll change my wardrobe next time.' She indicated her multi-coloured parka and neon trainers.

'Are you sure you don't mind being in economy while I'm flouncing around with the other half?'

'I'm happy with the plebs.'

'Well, I'm not going to the premier lounge. C'mon, let's have a pleb's full Scottish to celebrate.' Sandy checked her phone. 'The security info said it would take thirteen-and-a-half minutes to get through.'

'With a bit of luck, it'll only take 2.75 minutes to get to the restaurant, making it sixteen-and-a-quarter minutes in total until breakfast!'

They grinned and linked arms as they stepped onto the escalator.

***

Isobel's phone vibrated as Sandy gathered the empty plates and pushed them to the end of the table. 'Who's that at this time?'

'Och, I told the kids I would text before lift-off. They obviously can't wait.'

'I'm going to the loo, won't be long.' She took off, checking the announcement board on the way, making sure there were no delays or cancellations. Inside, she refreshed her make-up and re-pinned her hair, wetting an annoying tendril that refused to stay put.

Heading back to the table, Sandy could see her friend scanning the crowd with a worried expression on her face. 'Is everything OK?'

'Oh dear. I don't know how to say this.'

'What is it? Spit it out.'

'It's Chip.'

'What's happened?'

'I was texting with him last night about our trip, and he's only bought a ticket so he can be there too!'

Sandy crossed her arms. 'He hasn't. Really? This is meant to be our weekend!'

'I'm sorry,' Isobel said, but her face was flushed with excitement. 'I didn't expect him to book a flight, but I'd like to see him, if it's possible. Do you mind? Oh, I feel awful asking.'

Sandy's stomach churned with dismay, uncertain if she could handle Isobel's new man spending the entire weekend with them. 'Of course, I don't mind. I've only booked two tickets for each sightseeing, though.'

'He won't be around all weekend, I promise, but...'

Sandy could see how conflicted her friend was. 'Listen, I don't want to be a gooseberry either. Why don't you spend tomorrow with Chip, or rather, today? I'll be fine on my own.'

'It never dawned on me he would be so keen. I'll tell him to cancel; he shouldn't have done it. He can get a refund.'

Sandy clasped Isobel's hand. 'Listen, you have to meet him. You, more than anyone, know you have to take every opportunity in life, because we can't see the future. And I'll be fine.'

'Are you sure? Thank you Sandy, I mean it. Cripes, I haven't had sex in years. Thank God we booked separate rooms. And thank God I shaved; it was like the bloody Amazon down there. Please don't think me a bad friend.' Isobel made a circle with her finger pointing at her body. 'This is a desert. At least you're getting some.'

'I suppose. Believe me, it's nothing to write home about after all this time.'

'And you really don't mind?'

'I don't mind at all.' Although she did. She'd been relieved when Mike said he couldn't come and had been counting the days until the trip with Isobel, who was now deserting her as soon as they got there. But Isobel had been a solid friend to her since their schooldays, an angel through her toughest times and worked hard as a single mother with two teenage kids. She deserved some me-time.

Sandy examined her meticulous programme. 'So, we can get together again on Friday – an early start with the Met Gallery at 10 am. They say to allow two hours and I've added on an extra ten minutes to give us lee-way should we need it. And then it's a twenty-minute walk to The Sistina for our posh lunch.'

'That's my treat, remember.' Isobel looked up from the schedule. 'Thank you. I mean it. You are above and beyond.'

'We're off to New York to see The Brig. And you are going to have sex tonight, you lucky thing, you.'

‘I hope so. Can’t believe it,’ Isobel whispered. She looked back at the list. ‘OK, I have to ask. The bold? And the asterisks?’

‘Ah, yes, sorry, I should have explained. Bold is where it’s booked and ticketed. Two asterisks are where I’ve suggested a time, because it can’t be booked, so we may have to wait or come back later or something. Three asterisks are where I’ve suggested getting there early. Like for The Brig, doors open 7.30 pm. We could go earlier and queue to get a good spot. And these are only suggested getting up and going to bed times. I tried to work out the optimum we can do and still get the correct amount of sleep.’

Isobel scrutinised Sandy over the top of her glasses and raised her eyebrows.

‘Don’t say anything! It’s best to have a plan and if I don’t, it makes me…’ Sandy waggled her hands.

‘Out of control?’

‘Yeah. Out of control.’

Isobel touched her friend’s arm. ‘It will get easier with time.’

‘How much time? It’s been years.’

‘You’ll know.’ Isobel said gently. ‘There’ll be a day when things shift, and you can feel it, the pain is there but your response to it has altered. It will happen. Trust me, I’ve been there. And you’ve got Mike.’

Sandy read over her plans intently. She knew she might cry if she looked at her friend. She remembered the shock when Brian died so suddenly. Life could be flipped in an instant.

'Are you sure you're fine with being alone tomorrow? I mean today?' Isobel asked.

'Of course I am. A day of sightseeing on my own will be an adventure.' She said it with a conviction unmatched by her fears of being alone. She was happy for Isobel and a smidgen envious. She was going to meet someone new and her life was changing; whether it was with Chip or another man, she was sure her friend would be in another relationship soon. It might make things easier between them. She sensed a reticence in Isobel these days if she wanted to unload about her marriage to Mike. She didn't want to sound ungrateful; she still had a husband and Isobel had lost hers. She was lucky to have such a good man.

Her tummy was flipping at the unexpected change of plan. Perhaps time on her own could be a good thing, make her more independent. But she would cancel the restaurant; she didn't fancy eating alone. She whipped out her notebook and wrote *Cancel Oyster Bar* and added an asterisk. And, for good measure, she retrieved a Sharpie from her bag and made a large cross against the dinner on the schedule.

Eventually, the Edinburgh/Newark flight was called and they plodded forward with the other passengers at the gate. Sandy wrote a text to Mike telling him they were leaving on time and she'd been upgraded. Her finger hovered over the send button, then she erased it. He would be asleep anyway.

Isobel was reading another message on her mobile. 'Bloody hell. He's keen. He's meeting me at the airport 'cos his flight gets in about two hours before ours. Are you sure you don't mind me abandoning you?'

Sandy bit back a comment about what she thought of Chip right now and took a deep breath. 'It'll do me good. I've never done a trip on my own and besides, I'll see you tomorrow and you can regale me with salacious tales of your rendezvous with Chip.' She took out the laminated timetable; seeing it laid out before her was calming. She was so disappointed – and angry. 'Let's say goodbye here. We'll be coming off separately and it might be awkward if I'm there when you meet him. Three's a crowd!'

Isobel gave Sandy a squashy hug and whispered in her ear, 'Thank you for letting me do this.' Sandy kissed her cheek and squeezed back. She moved forward to the top of the queue and with her First Class ticket was ushered away from Isobel.

CHAPTER 4

How the other half live, Sandy mused as she was shown to her single seating area, impressed by the luxury. Thank you, Isobel! She shook out the complimentary pyjamas and slippers, anticipating a good sleep. She was about to take her seat when her hair was plucked in the opposite direction and she was dragged back down the aisle trying to save it.

'Owww!' The perpetrator was impervious to his catch; Sandy's hair was locked on the buckle of a guitar case. She grasped her head, too late to save a long coil being wrenched out and swung, still attached to the buckle, into the overhead locker of the single seating pod behind her. The man's ears were blocked with headphones, obliterating her angry yelps.

'Thank you very much!' she shouted in his direction, still ignored as he removed a battered leather jacket and pushed it into the locker. So much for premier class, the man was a tramp, with unkempt grey hair barely caught in an absurd flowery man-bun, and a ludicrous long beard. He was wearing a kilt, showing off beefy calves that would have been better hidden in denim.

An antique Aran jumper completed the rustic ensemble. Sandy glowered, giving him the evil eye as he calmly took his seat.

'For God's sake!' Sandy tried to sooth her stinging head, her eyes watering with the pain. She settled into her own space, determined not to let the assault spoil her enjoyment of the unexpected grandeur, appreciating the luxurious free extras and admiring the ergonomic design of the pod. She hung her jacket and placed her shoes on a shelf. She popped on the complimentary slippers and went to the loo – much larger than any previous airline convenience she'd come across – where she got into the pyjamas that had been placed on her seat. It was nearly 5 am and she was ready for a good sleep. She brushed her hair gingerly, a small bare patch evidence of her neighbour's disregard, before pinning it away. Once ready for bed, she scurried back to her seat and happily folded her trousers over the hanger and hung them beside her jacket.

As she extended her seat into a full-length bed, she had a momentary pang of guilt as she imagined Isobel in cramped economy. Then she remembered her chum was about to have a romantic encounter, something Sandy had hoped to spark with Mike when she'd initially asked him to come. She sensed she and her husband were drifting, parallel but apart, and was unsure how to regain the closeness they once had. And here she was, more alone than ever.

'Would you like something to drink before we take off, ma'am?'

'Still water please.'

The steward breaking into her thoughts hadn't stopped the frustration beginning to surface. She'd resigned from her job six months ago so they could take time off and travel, yet Mike remained employed. Promises to hand in his notice were always broken for one reason or another. They had plans to travel the world, have an adventure, and tick off their bucket list destinations as they went. New York was one of them. How was it going to work if she'd been and he hadn't? Did it mean they had to make a return visit? Would Mike miss it from his list? The steward brought the water and immediately Sandy regretted not ordering a large gin instead.

The lights were lowered in the cabin and the plane took off. Sandy soon dozed, the nipping of her scalp where the hair had been wrenched out reduced to a mild ache.

Within half an hour she was awake, disturbed by the rear passenger's light flooding on as he asked for a whisky, with water on the side. Next, she was disturbed by his mumbled singing, unrecognisable fragments bringing her out of any snatched slumber. Sandy put on the eye mask and ear plugs and was dropping off when she was woken again, this time by something tickling her face. She lifted her mask to see her neighbour's feet, in thick woolly socks, had squashed themselves through to the side of her seat and were wiggling close to her face.

'Can you believe this!' Sandy turned over so her head faced the opposite way, put her ear pods in and selected The Brig's ballad album from her phone. None of it did any good, there was no respite from the old, kilted neighbour who was up and down during the night and inevitably grasped heavily on to her seat back, shuddering her awake if she did manage to drop off.

CHAPTER 5

'Sandy? Sandy?'

She felt as though she'd only been asleep for two minutes when she woke to her friend shaking her shoulder. 'I wanted to say cheerio,' said Isobel. 'We'll be landing soon.'

Sandy sat up and rubbed her eyes. 'You look gorgeous!' And she did – her friend's glossy brunette hair was attractively held in an easy updo. Her makeup was flawless, including bright red lipstick, matching a red top.

'Thank you. Comes with having a teenage daughter. How was your night in here? I had the best sleep I've had in years, and the attendant let me use the first class bathroom to get ready when I told her about Chip.'

'I'm sorry, Madam, you'll have to return to your seat as we'll be starting our descent soon.' A steward began ushering Isobel towards economy.

'OK, I'll go. See you tomorrow.'

Sandy was groggy and put out that Isobel should have had such a great sleep when hers had been a nightmare. She stood but had to swerve out of the way, as her neighbour made a badly plotted lunge for the loo, almost falling in the door. Sandy trotted off to the other one at the front of the cabin, She brushed her teeth, had a quick wet wipe bath and replaced her underwear with a fresh set. Her suit was in perfect condition. Now she understood why the rich and famous were so glamorous and uncrumpled when they were spotted coming off a flight.

Despite the dreadful night, she recognised an excitement she hadn't had for years, tinged with fear at spending an entire day and night in a strange place on her own. As they landed, she checked the time, delighted the plane had arrived on schedule. If she could get through passport control quickly and onto the AirTrain, it would then be less than sixty minutes before she arrived at the hotel. Relieved she'd left plenty of leeway, she realised she might even be ahead of herself. How satisfying. She stood, ready to leave the plane.

'Can you help me...please?,' a voice slurred in her direction. Sandy recoiled as she found the kilt man breathing whisky fumes over her, as he floundered to stay on his feet. He leaned in with a scrunched-up face as if experiencing difficulty forcing the words out, and when they came, he mumbled, 'My legs aren't working.' He veered in the opposite direction and automatically Sandy grabbed his jumper to stop him falling. He was held in space for a moment, until she managed to hoist him upright.

'I'm sho...shorry.' He groaned, then stared at her intently. 'Why do I shound like Sean Connery?'

'What's the matter with you?'

He'd managed to entangle his guitar case with the shoulder bag and had trapped his arms. Sandy spent some time extricating him as passengers manoeuvred around them.

'I think I'm drunk.'

'You sound shocked. Something to do with the whisky you had?' Sandy was frustrated to have this cumbersome, unpleasant person draped over her. She managed to balance him, as the last passenger squeezed past. A steward appeared, a different one from the night before.

'Do you need help with hubby?'

'He's not my husband.' Sandy was appalled at the suggestion.

'OK. No judgement here. I'll help you off with him.'

'But...'

The steward had already taken one side, and Sandy was obliged to manage her own bags in one hand and take the weight of the man on her other side.

'Come on now. Let's get you off the plane, sir.'

'I'm so sorry.'

At least he was apologetic she thought sourly as they stepped off the plane.

'First Class border control to the left. Bye!'

The steward let go, leaving Sandy and the nincompoop – as she was now calling him in her head – to go careening into the wall, flattening her against the side.

'Help me...please.'

'Is that all you can say?' She steadied herself and pushed away from the wall, bringing her nurse training into her body. The nincompoop held on to her and they staggered forward. Underneath the whisky she could smell a slight spice and musky scent, not unpleasant, and although his clothes appeared well worn they weren't dirty. Sandy aimed them towards border control, some way off.

'Where's your passport? They'll never let you in if you're this drunk. Act sober!'

Kilt Man took a deep breath and rallied himself to his full height. 'It's in my bag.' A drunken hand was trying to open the leather strap. Sandy stopped, laid him against the wall and swiped his hand out of the way, delving into the bag to find a passport.

'I'm sorry.'

'Oh, stop saying sorry, you fool.' She got her own passport out and opened it to the photo page then did the same with the stranger's. She closed it and opened it again; was she hallucinating?

She wasn't.

The name on the passport was Jake Cabrelli. She scrutinised the photo. Oh My God. Could it be? She examined the wreck slumped against the wall beside her, then pushed away his hair and gazed at his face. Moving in closer, she propped an eyelid open and an icy blue pupil sparked out from the red surrounding it.

She drew away, horrified. 'Oh my God! You are Jake Cabrelli!'

He lifted his hand and hit his head in mock salute, promptly falling sideways. They were still hidden by the small queue in front but it was slowly disappearing and Jake's condition would be revealed. His eyes had closed and she feared he was going to sleep.

‘OK, if you want to get into the US you need to pull yourself together.’ Her attempts to prise him from the wall were unsuccessful and she was conscious of the dwindling numbers hiding them from view of border control. Sandy slammed her sensible shoe on his foot.

‘Owww! What did you do that for?’ Jake had the cheek to be resentful, although it had brought him out of the stupor. They lurched towards the desk.

‘I'm sorry, my friend didn't sleep well on the plane; he's a bit disoriented.’

The solemn-faced officer took their passports. ‘Ya shoudda had another photo done with that beard and hair. It's outta control, man.’ He examined the documents. ‘Jake Cabrelli. Why is your name familiar? Didn't you used to be somebody?’

Jake took a breath to speak but it became a yawn.

‘He's a musician,’ Sandy explained, hoping it might excuse the state of him.

‘OK. Get in front of the scanner. Lady, move the hair out of his eyes.’

Sandy did as instructed, contorting herself over their luggage. ‘Keep still,’ she said as she managed to hold Jake's head in place.

‘Fingers next. On the machine here.’

Sandy wedged Jake's fingers flat on the little box. After a few false starts the officer had the images he needed. ‘OK. Ma'am, you next.’

Sandy moved forward and with some difficulty, as she was still holding the nincompoop, her scan and fingerprints were taken and the officer opened the automatic door to let them pass.

'I'm not a smuggler. You could smile.' Jake slurred and his head lolled as he offered his hand to the officer. Sandy snatched his hand away and took the passports.

'Shut up. He's letting us in!' She led a wobbling Jake through to the other side and miraculously they went unchallenged at Customs. Bracing herself, she took the weight of her former idol as they stumbled along an endless corridor and past the baggage reclaim area. She had a quick search for Isobel but couldn't see her. A huge *Welcome To The* USA sign appeared overhead and they reeled through the sliding doors. Further on, Sandy dumped him on an airport chair in the arrivals hall and he immediately crashed out.

'I have to leave you here.' Sandy stared at him. This was weird. Jake Cabrelli, a drunken shambles in front of her and looking as if he'd been lost in Patagonia for years. She couldn't do anything else. He'd sleep it off, get himself together and go on to wherever he was going, and she would see him on Saturday night from the audience. She looked around in the hope some form of help might materialise but the only person close by was a man in a smart suit with short dreads holding a sign up saying 'Mr Ginsberg'.

Jake snored. His wallet fell from his jacket and hit the floor, a wad of cash tumbling out. Hundreds of dollars. *He's a liability*, she thought as she picked it up.

'Where are you going?' She prodded his shoulder. Nothing. Tapped his cheek. No response. With a quick glance around she slammed on his foot again.

He came to and shook his head. 'What?'

'I've got a boat booked to the Statue of Liberty, so help me out here. Where are you going?' Sandy bellowed at him. He may be Jake Cabrelli but she had a timetable.

'The hotel. My foot hurts.'

Sandy tucked his wallet into his pocket and he sank back in the seat, eyes closed, lost to the world. By this time, his guitar case was round his neck, in danger of throttling him. As Sandy deliberated her options, Jake slipped further in the chair and the wallet hit the floor a second time.

This weekend had not started happily. She snatched the wallet, then took the seat beside him. He was off his face. Is this the life he'd chosen – an alcoholic vagrant? Albeit a posh one travelling First Class and he obviously had cash, but how had he come to this state?

She switched her mobile on and scoured the arrivals hall hoping to see Isobel, but she was nowhere to be seen, just the occasional straggling passenger. There was no signal on her phone and she kept refreshing to see if the network would kick in. Nothing.

She regarded the ungainly heap and sighed. For old times' sake she couldn't leave him behind. She put her own bag across her body and managed to secure the guitar case across his chest. Rolling her carry-on into position, she hauled Jake off the seat, and while navigating the bags, lugged him in the direction of taxis.

'Where are you staying?'

No response. She eyed the long taxi queue from across the road, not relishing holding Jake upright for an extended period of time. No sign of Isobel in the queue either. She was about to step onto the road when she saw the suited man from earlier exit the arrivals hall and throw his 'Mr Ginsberg' sign in the bin.

'Excuse me. Excuse me.' She dragged Jake as the man turned.

'Yeah, lady?'

'Are you a driver? I saw you with the sign and putting it in the bin and...'

The man eyed Jake warily and then back at Sandy. 'Where do you wanna go?'

'To my hotel, 34th Street. We can pay you – cash. He's got... we've got cash.'

The man's eyes flicked across to the taxi rank and back. 'Two hundred bucks.'

Sandy knew the fare in a yellow cab would be half that, but she didn't care. She had no intention of paying. 'Yes. Yes, please.'

'Follow me.' The man moved off and Sandy followed, struggling with an intricate path between rows of cars until the driver fired a key fob and lights flashed on a black sedan in the distance. 'Gimme your case.' Sandy gratefully passed it over. 'It's illegal to pick up unbooked like this so...'

They reached the car and the man opened the passenger door. Jake tried to clamber in but the guitar case across his body prevented access.

‘Hey fella. That’s not gonna work.’ The driver swivelled him round.

‘I’m sorry, he had a few sherries on the plane.’

The driver examined Jake’s face holding his beard to keep him in place. ‘Looks loaded on somethin’ to me.’ He extricated him from the strap.

‘It’s my guitar, man. You can’t take my guitar.’ Jake waved uselessly in the air.

‘I’m not stealing your guitar, trying to help you, old buddy.’

Sandy placed her case in the trunk, depositing Jake's guitar on top. Jake crawled in the back and crashed out, taking up most of the space. A real gent. She squeezed in beside him and the driver eased the sedan out of the parking space.

CHAPTER 6

'I'm sorry, I've no idea where he's going, I kind of got saddled with him.' Jake's mouth was wide and drooling. 'He's drunk.' She leant over and opened the window.

'Are you sure he's not taken anything?'

'I'm not sure.' Sandy put her head in her hands.

'OK. I'm sorry, lady, but you both gotta get out at the same place 'cos you can't leave him with me, not in this state. So where's you headin' exactly, ma'am?'

She wished Mike were here, he'd know how to resolve this. Or Isobel – at least they could have a laugh about it. She was in a taxi with Jake Cabrelli!

'I want to go to the City Hotel, East 34th and Lexington please.' She said it like a local and it made her feel slightly better even when she considered her predicament. Everything was going to be fine. They exited the car park and were soon snaking their way out of the airport. The driver fiddled with some buttons and Latin-sounding rhythms escaped the speakers.

'Juan Luis Guerra!' Jake sat up. 'I love his music!' He peered at the company sign above the sunshade. 'Great taste, Roberto.'

‘I ain’t Roberto; my name’s Jonjo.’

The effort of speaking had been too much and Jake resumed his slumped position. ‘At least he’s got a good taste in music,’ said the driver.

‘He used to be a guitarist in a band.’

Sandy gazed at the passing cityscape. The April sun was shining and checking her phone, she could see they might be cutting it fine for her to get to the Tick Tock diner but there was still plenty time to catch the boat. Statue of Liberty, here I come – as long as she could get rid of her passenger. She watched the sleeping Jake. Whoever said you should never meet your heroes had it right. The famous skyline came into view, but it went unnoticed as Sandy wracked her brain for a solution. As the car drove into the Lincoln Tunnel, she deliberated rifling through his bag. He may have a printout of hotel detail or something. As she moved his hand off the closure, he hugged the bag to him making access impossible. Then inspiration struck. Easy! She’d get him a room at her hotel; he had plenty cash. She could leave him to sleep it off and resume her weekend. There was always a solution.

The car came up into the bright sunlight and was immediately snarled in traffic, a cacophony of horns filling the air, the drivers making everyone aware of their displeasure. Jake slept on. As the sea of vehicles inched forward Sandy’s impression was of chaos – noisy engines, building works, crowded pavements. Jonjo confidently weaved a route and eventually drew in to the kerb outside the hotel. 'Here we are, ma'am. Now, what are you gonna do 'bout him, as I can't take him?'

'If you can help me get him out, I'll book him a room here. I sort of know him, or know who he is, so it'll be fine.'

Jonjo levered Jake out of the car while Sandy gathered their luggage, slamming the boot shut. 'I'm sorry about this and I'm so grateful for the lift.' Jonjo held him while she got herself together.

'Are you sure you're gonna be OK, ma'am? Is there someone you can call?'

'My friend should be here soon and she'll help.'

'The amount of times I used to get stuck with drunks in a cab. It's why I do car service these days, less intoxication goin' on.'

Sandy paid him from Jake's wallet, giving him a generous tip.

'Thanks!'

'Thank him.' Sandy gestured to Jake.

Jonjo helped her to the entrance of the hotel and propped Jake against the wall. 'Good luck!'

The sedan whizzed off and Sandy got everything together again. Pulling Jake off the wall, she managed to squish them into the revolving door. It took three tries to get out and she was grateful to a guest who put their foot in the door to stop it. She pushed the zombified Jake onto a chair in reception and went to the desk. 'I'd like to check in please. Stuart. I booked two rooms, with early check in. And I'd like to book another room for my friend here.' Sandy indicated behind her. Jake had slumped across two chairs. 'He's tired. Been travelling a while.' She dashed over and tried to sit him up as a small bottle fell from his jacket. Sandy stuck it in her pocket.

'We're fully booked. Can I have your passport, please?' She searched around in her bag. Both passports should be together. She remembered they were still in her hand when she put everything in the boot. Oh Lord! Horrified, she realised she must have put the passports in with the cases and left them there.

'I can't believe it; I've left our passports in the taxi. I've paid for the rooms – could you take my driving licence as ID until I can get them?' Could Jake be dumped in Isobel's room until a solution presented itself? She could make herself scarce and the lovebirds could have her room and...

'Driving licence is fine, so don't worry, ma'am. We've seen your friend's passport, she's in her room and we have her card impression, so if you give me your credit card, we'll be fine and dandy.'

Isobel was already here? How much time had been wasted helping Jake? A quick glance at the reception wall clock told her it was 10.25am; there was no way she'd make the Tick Tock brunch booking now.

'And for my friend here? Is there nothing at all?' Sandy pointed at Jake who was sitting with his head lolled to the side, mouth wide and snoring like a lord.

'Your room is a double, ma'am. Perhaps he could stay with you?'

'But he's not my husband.'

'It's OK, madam. We don't mind.'

She could dump him in her room with a note and still make the Statue of Liberty cruise. Inhaling deeply, Sandy accepted the key card, and replacing the guitar case across her body, walked over to Jake. She shook him. No response. Then shook him harder. Nothing. Turning to see if anyone was watching she stamped her shoe on his boot.

'Aaargh. What was that for?'

'C'mon, we have to go.' With her free hand she hefted him and aimed for the lift. With difficulty she manoeuvred him out again and into the hotel room, where he moved forward, zombie-like, and fell face front onto the bed.

Sandy dumped the bags and sat on one of the easy chairs. This trip was jinxed. Something was poking into her bottom and she took out the bottle that had fallen earlier.

'Fifteen Day Ultimate Weight Loss. Cleanse and Flush.'

'Good grief!' She was shocked at the ingredients. Phenolphthalein – she was familiar with it from work. It was banned. And Sibutramine – withdrawn. Why is he taking these? There was more on the list she didn't recognise. No surprise he was off his face. She opened the bottle and a single yellow tablet fell out. How many had he taken today? Should she put him in the recovery position? Sibutramine could cause a stroke. He was a big guy and overweight, although it was difficult to tell exactly his size with the chunky knitted jumper and kilt. Sandy went over to the bed and watched him. He was sleeping soundly, clutching his bag like a frightened pensioner. She went into nurse mode.

'C'mon.' She lifted him into a sitting position. 'We need to get this bag off you.'

'No,' he moaned, 'not my bag.'

'It's fine. You're safe here.'

Jake let her gently remove his bag and she took the leather jacket off. He would be overheating in the jumper but she couldn't extricate it from his body. The well-splattered front told the story of the times he hadn't connected his mouth with the whisky. Sandy lifted his jumper and saw how tight his kilt was around his midriff. She found the makeshift ties and loosened them off, then removed his boots, bewildered at how the day had unfolded.

'I am undressing Jake Cabrelli,' she said to no-one.

'I'm so sorry.' The patient mumbled from the bed and she heaved him onto his side, his belly spilling free from the kilt. This was not the sex god of her schoolgirl fantasies.

Sandy reduced the air con and sat on the easy chair, watching him breathing. There was no way she could leave him. He might have a stroke. Or a heart attack. What had he been thinking? What had happened to this man who had made teenagers swoon – had made her swoon? Had he been living in a cave – and dining on illegal slimming pills?

She took her schedule out of her bag, and dug in again, bringing out the Sharpie. She put a big black cross beside the brunch, and with a deep sigh, the pen hovered over the Statue of Liberty. So much for her itinerary. She settled in the chair with her mobile, which had a signal at last, and googled car service companies.

CHAPTER 7

'Argh!'

Sandy woke abruptly at the noise, her hands still clutching the mobile.

'Who are you? Why are you in my hotel room?' Jake pulled the bed cover across him, like an innocent starlet caught naked.

'This is my hotel room, and you were so drunk on the plane, I got stuck with getting you out of the airport. You couldn't make any sense, so I had to bring you here.'

'Were we drinking together?'

'No. You did it all on your own.'

Jake sat up. 'Where's my bag?' He patted the bed covers.

'It's on the floor beside you.'

He picked it up and held it to him. 'Is this New York?'

'Yes, it is.'

'And you are?'

'Sandy Stuart. Fellow passenger on the flight from Edinburgh to Newark.'

Jake took a moment. 'I remember being at the airport. I can't remember getting on the plane. Is this a scam?'

'Nope.'

Jake retrieved his jacket and checked the pockets. 'Where's my wallet?'

Sandy flung it and he deftly caught it. 'It's a bit light because I decided it was only fair you paid for the taxi.'

He winced. 'I'm sorry.'

'So you kept saying earlier. Or it was more "I'm shorry".'

'I am sorry. I don't usually get so drunk that I don't remember.'

'It's probably because you were taking these.' She pitched the pill bottle to him. 'Why do you have these tablets? They're dangerous.'

Jake missed the bottle and bent to pick it up. 'Well, this is embarrassing.'

'More embarrassing than having to be helped into a stranger's hotel room?'

'Kind of.'

'At least you're awake and not in a coma, so we can go our separate ways.'

'Why didn't you wake me?'

Sandy glared at him. She'd missed half her day and he was being an ungrateful toad.

'OK. OK. I get it. You tried.'

'You think you've wasted time? I should be boarding a ferry for the Statue of Liberty and Ellis Island about now. The booking for brunch at Tick Tock is well past. Not to mention I've got a lump on my head where your guitar case wrenched my hair out!'

Jake grimaced. 'Really?'

Sandy nodded towards the offending case where the evidence could still be seen. 'Yes. Really.'

Jake delicately undid the hair from the buckle and hesitated before handing it to her. Sandy raised an eyebrow and he laid the strands on the pillow.

'I'm so sorry.'

'Stop saying sorry!'

He stood and had to grab at the kilt as it fell to the floor. Horrified, he gathered it to him. 'I didn't expose myself did I?'

'No. You didn't. You were a well-behaved, extremely inebriated person.'

He eyed Sandy suspiciously as he tied his kilt. 'You didn't interfere with me, did you?'

'No! Why would you think that?'

'There are a lot of strange people in the world.' He put his boots on. 'My feet hurt. Weird!'

Sandy looked away, her face hot.

'Do you mind if I ask you where my suitcase is?'

'I had no idea you even had one.'

Jake put on his jacket and gathered his belongings together. 'Thank you, Sandy. I'm sure I owe you a lot more than a thank you. I'm Jake by the way.'

'I know who you are, I had to get you through passport control. Passports! Oh my God. I forgot about the passports. They're in the taxi.'

Jake sank onto the bed. 'You left them in the taxi?'

'Not on purpose, you bloody nincompoop!'

'Ah, nincompoop. From the 1670s I believe. Connected to non compos mentis.'

'What are you on about? We have to concentrate on getting our passports.'

'I was trying to lighten the mood.'

'Well don't. OK? Oh God, I can't remember the name of the car company!'

'Yellow cabs by any chance?'

'Haha. No! It was a black sedan who gave us a lift when their own passenger didn't show up.'

'That helps a lot. Didn't you check the name of the company – could've been anybody, we might have been kidnapped!'

'I had other things on my mind. Why don't you make yourself useful and google a list of car services, instead of being sarky?' Sandy wheeled her case to the bathroom. 'His name was Jonjo, and it was a private car service company I think. Very smart suit – that's it! Slick Service. It was on the name card with 'Roberto'. Try them.'

She closed the door behind her and after a quick wash, dressed in a smart pair of camel trousers with matching blazer and a fresh cream blouse. They were crumpled despite the tissue. Sandy brushed her hair and winced as she passed over the bald spot. She pinned it tightly into a French knot. As she re-applied her make-up she stopped and mouthed 'Jake Cabrelli' to her reflection, shaking her head. She came out of the bathroom as he was finishing on the phone.

'Any luck?'

'Unbelievably, yes. They're at the depot in Brooklyn, near Prospect Park.'

'OK, let's go.'

Jake walked towards her but after a few steps he lurched to the left, holding his head and dropped on to a chair.

'Are you OK?'

'Dizzy.' He was pale under the beard and hair.

'When was the last time you actually ate anything?'

'Umm, I can't remember.'

Sandy opened the fridge and handed a bottle of water to Jake. 'Yesterday?'

'I'm not sure, I've been on a health-kick fasting thing.'

'With those tablets? You need food before we do anything.'

'I'm not sure I can eat.'

'You don't diet by starving yourself, taking pills and drinking alcohol. You need proper food.' She glanced at the room service menu.

'Only available after 5pm – not much of a service.' She walked toward him. 'Give me the guitar.'

'You are so bossy.'

'Do you have any suggestions?' Sandy wrestled it over her body.

'Let's leave it here and I'll come back for it once we have the passports? It'll be much easier than taking it to Brooklyn.' She laid it carefully on the bed then took his elbow to support him.

'I'm like a character in a Bronte novel. Somebody with consumption.'

'It's your lack of consumption that got you here. C'mon.'

CHAPTER 8

They spun through the revolving door more successfully than before and Sandy's senses were immediately assaulted by Manhattan. She hadn't noticed earlier while her focus had been on a drunk man with a guitar. The air smelled of hot fried donuts, with undertones of rotting food; the sound of roadworks filled the air, mixing with the traffic. The street was busy in the middle of the day and the two of them created an island pedestrians had to navigate as they tried to find their bearings. Sandy put her hands over her ears and craned her neck to take in the height of the skyscrapers, seeing the sky blue and clear above. The energy from the city pulsated through her body. A cool breeze was fresh against her skin after so long inside, and as she deciphered birdsong amidst the clamour, she came back to reality. She glanced at Jake who appeared equally discombobulated.

'Let's go this way and stop at any half-decent place to eat.' Sandy headed east on 34th Street, Jake shuffling beside her. The area was full of tall apartment buildings but a bright banner in an alley caught her eye as it fluttered in the light wind. It proclaimed, 'Kitty's Diner' and she led them towards a human-sized hotdog holding a weather-worn menu promising the best all-day breakfasts, comfort classics and cheesy melts. 'This'll do.'

Jake followed her in.

Seated in a booth, under the spell of the restaurant's aroma, her tummy rumbled. There'd been nothing since the airport breakfast as she'd refused the in-flight meals in her desire for sleep. Jake sat with his head in his hands as she read the menu and the waiter arrived with glasses and poured water.

'What will you folks be having today?'

'I'll have a triple stack, with syrup, bacon, sausage—'

'Hold on. You said you were on a diet and you can't have a triple stack after you've eaten nothing for ages.' She turned to the waiter. 'He'll have scrambled eggs, mushrooms, small portion of hash browns and one slice of ham. In fact, I'll have the same. Lots more water, please.'

Jake glared at her as the waiter wrote down their order. 'OK Matron! Do people always do what you say?'

'Only when I'm right.'

'I can look after myself if you don't mind. I was trying to lose a bit of weight for a special occasion.' He sat there, his hair a fright, stomach stretching the cabled jumper.

'I know who you are.'

'Yes. You saw my passport.'

'You're Jake Cabrelli, founding member of The Brig.'

Jake clutched his face in faux horror. 'You're a deranged fan who wants to make me healthy for some bizarre sacrifice!'

'And you're a clod who can't see when someone's trying to help you.'

'Ah, clod. A magnificent sixteenth-century insult. A stupid person, blockhead, dolt.'

'You said it.' Sandy straightened her cutlery and table mat so they sat symmetrically, moving on to arrange the condiments.

'Does it make you feel better? Getting everything exact and in place?' He poked a fork towards the table manoeuvres and tipped over the salt.

She tutted and righted it then trapped her hands under her thighs. 'Why go on a crash diet?'

'I couldn't get into my old clothes.'

'Why didn't you buy new ones? That would be the sensible thing to do.'

'Well, Miss Sensible, I wanted to wear clothes from previous concerts, since you know so much about me.'

'And you imagined you were going to be the same size?' Sandy snorted.

'Ah, Miss Perfection, I should have called you. I bet you've never been on a diet in your life.'

She scowled at him. 'I wouldn't be foolish enough to take life-threatening useless slimming tablets. You only had to read the ingredients to see how dangerous it was.'

'I never read the ingredients of anything.'

'Not even whisky?

'I bet you're some sort of penpusher – so precise, with your timetables and ingredient obsession and smart suits. No place for the less perfect of the world.'

'I'm an academic actually.'

'Ha! I knew it.'

The waiter came with their food and placed heaving plates in front of them.

'An academic is not a penpusher,' she said. 'And at least I can hold my drink. When I drink.'

'I'm happy I made you feel superior by getting drunk and disorderly,' Jake sniped.

'So I should have left you in the airport to get robbed? I didn't want to give up my day for you.'

'I can't imagine you giving up anything for anyone. Bossy Boots.'

Sandy was exasperated. 'You don't even know me!'

Jake put his head in his hands. 'I'm sorry. I'm a hungover ass, and obviously hangry.' He wiped his hands over his face. 'Can we start again?'

Sandy eyed him belligerently.

'Hello. I'm Jake Cabrelli and I'm extremely grateful you got me off the flight, with my bag and guitar, got me through passport control and into New York City. I'm sorry I'm an idiot and your day has been ruined.' He held out his hand. 'Forgive me?'

After a few seconds she took his hand and shook it, although she was still bristling inside at the penpusher comment. They concentrated on their meals, Jake tucking in with gusto. Sandy, astonished by the amount of food in front of her, scooped up some scrambled egg.

'You don't look terribly overweight,' she said. 'That jumper and the beard have a lot to answer for and everyone puts weight on as they get older. It's natural.'

Jake lifted his water to toast Sandy and drank it before refilling their glasses. 'I thought we were starting over?'

'I'm telling you the facts. For the future.'

'I don't need the facts. I'm capable of taking care of myself.'

'Could've fooled me.' Sandy took out her schedule and examined it.

'A laminated schedule? That's not the way to see a city. You've got to leave room for the unexpected.'

'Like this, you mean?' Sandy flapped her napkin between them and at the breakfast. 'I've always wanted to see the Statue of Liberty – it's been on my list for years. And now...'

'Can't you fit it in somewhere else?'

'No. I've made my plans and there's other things I've organised. I didn't expect to deal with a uselessly drunk passenger.'

'You should have left me, I would've managed.'

'You weren't managing this morning. You were begging for help when you were legless – literally!'

Sandy concentrated on her phone, using Google to work out how long it might take to get to Brooklyn and return to the hotel, marking times in her notebook.

Jake stabbed his knife towards the schedule. 'Not exactly a seasoned traveller, are you? Doing it by the book, safe and secure with your smart suit and sensible shoes. And your cast-iron timetable.'

'I can do what I like when I like and if I want to alter my timetable I will. I'm free as a bird.' God, the man was insufferable and brought out the worst in her. There was no way she was telling him she was here for the concert – she would give her ticket to Chip. He was such a jerk. ‘Why don’t you turn your smarty-pants observational skills on yourself? You look like you’ve been hiding in a basement for years, a frightened rabbit. Mr Has Been Pop Star, who used to be somebody. Now you’re Mr Nobody - on your ownio ‘cos no one can bear being with you.’

The expression on Jake’s face told Sandy her insult had hit home and she felt sick with regret at being so cruel.

He pushed his plate away. ‘You’re right. I have been a bit of a recluse. Not sure how to function in society anymore, as you are aware. I apologise.’ He crumpled his napkin into a ball and threw it on his plate. ‘I’ll get the bill and we can grab a cab to Brooklyn. Then you can continue with your schedule.’ He paused. ‘But I would like to point out, it was you who left the passports in the boot.’

Outside the diner Jake put his thumb and forefinger in his mouth and emitted a loud whistle. Sandy couldn’t help but be impressed when a taxi immediately zigzagged across the traffic lanes towards them. They were soon winding their way towards Brooklyn. She stared out of the window at the city and despite the uncomfortable situation, was thrilled to be there, taking photos and videos as they motored through Manhattan. ‘It’s like being in a movie. I didn’t think it would feel so...freeing to be in such a huge place.

Jake watched her as she took in as much as she could from the window, her enthusiasm infectious. ‘It’s the energy, it thrums with life. I’d forgotten how it felt, to be here. To live here.’

'You lived in New York?'

'For ten years.' He opened the window. 'Madison Square Gardens is over there.' Sandy swivelled in the seat to see. 'And if you crane your neck you can see the Empire State Building too. I imagine that's on your list?'

'Of course. Noon, Sunday.' Sandy's head whirled as she tried to take in the sights.

'The Flatiron Building? It's in that direction.'

'No. There wasn't enough time.'

'You should, it's iconic – a triangular shaped skyscraper.'

They drove onto the Manhattan Bridge and Sandy could see the wide, choppy waters of the East River.

'There!' Jake pointed out from his window. 'The Statue of Liberty. It was on your list and now you can cross it off 'cos you've seen it.'

Sandy leaned past and could see the tiny figure, beyond the Brooklyn Bridge. 'It's not quite the same though is it – I need binoculars!'

'Dumbo.'

She glowered at him. 'Excuse me?'

'Down under the Manhattan Bridge Overpass. Dumbo. It's a great neighbourhood – is that on your list?'

'I've never heard of it.'

'I lived there for a while.' Jake gazed out at the area and they sat in silence until the driver pulled up outside the Slick Service Cars depot.

CHAPTER 9

'Jonjo's not here and there's nuthin' about any passports.' The woman behind the desk pushed herself backwards in a wheelchair, and expertly revolved 180 degrees as she arrived at a wall of hooks at the back of the depot office. 'Keys are here. Who told you he left passports?' Sandy felt a wave of despair come over her.

'A guy I spoke to on the phone said Jonjo was going to leave them.' answered Jake.

'Bill? He had to leave early, some emergency. I'm usually on nights, haven't had a chance to get goin' with nuthin' yet.' This time the chair sailed to the other end of the office and the woman, whose name badge declared her to be Cheryl, rummaged through drawers. 'There's nuthin' here.'

'Would they still be in the car?' Jake asked.

Cheryl spoke into a walkie talkie. 'Mohammed?' The radio crackled and a faint 'Yup' could be heard from the other end. 'Did you find anything left in 213 when you cleaned?'

'Nope.'

She waggled the radio at them. 'Nuthin'.'

'Did he clean the boot?' Sandy asked, and seeing Cheryl's quizzical brow added, 'The trunk?'

'Mohammed?'

'Yup.'

'Did you check the trunk?'

'Yup.'

'And nuthin'?'

'Nuthin'.'

Cheryl replaced the radio on the counter. 'Nuthin'.' Seeing their dismay she took pity. 'Let me call him and get the lowdown.'

'Thank you.' Sandy took a seat and tried to be patient while Cheryl punched in numbers with a pen, her nails far too long and intricately decorated to be used for the purpose.

'Jonjo, it's Cheryl. At the depot. Folks are here for passports. Call me.' She replaced the receiver. 'No luck, people, he's not picking up.'

'We need our passports.' Sandy came back to the counter. 'Do you know where he might be?' She had visions of this taking all day. 'I'm only here for the weekend, and I've got appointments and a flight back to Scotland. I need my passport.'

Cheryl shook her head. 'He lives local, but I can't be handing out addresses to any candyass crusty coming in here.'

'He's in a band!'

'I'm mighty happy for ya but that's nuthin' to do with anything. My brother's in a band.'

'I mean he's famous. Or used to be.'

'Hey, watch it!' Jake said.

Sandy tapped away on her phone and a picture of The Brig in earlier days appeared. She brandished it at Cheryl. 'See.'

'Which one are you?'

'There. At the front.' Jake said proudly, pointing at his younger self.

'Are you yanking ma chain?'

'No, it's me, in The Brig. Have you heard "Goodbye?"' Jake sang a line from their worldwide hit and Cheryl's fingers expanded the picture on Sandy's phone.

'Mister, you have let yourself go.' She drummed her fingernails on the counter while pondering. 'Let me see when he's next on shift.' She tapped into the keys again and a huge chart came on screen. 'Sunday. Leave me your number and I'll pass it to him.'

Sandy tried to see into the screen but Jake moved and blocked her view. Annoyed, she peeked from behind. 'I could leave my phone as collateral. I mean I need it, it's got my tickets and everything on it, so you'd be confident I wouldn't run off.'

'Lady, I ain't giving you his address. You don't look like serial killers, but who knows? The beardman here is wearing a strange skirt.'

'I only arrived in the US this morning and—'

Jake interrupted Sandy. 'Wow Cheryl, is that you holding a 300-strike trophy?'

She propelled herself towards a large photograph on the wall where she was front and centre of a group of wheelchair users, holding a cup aloft. 'Sure is. Two years ago now, but we're gonna do it again this year. You play?'

'You bet, never hit 300 though.'

Sandy shook her head at his timewasting. 'Is there nothing you can do to help?'

'It's cool – here's my number, please pass it on when Jonjo calls.' Jake scribbled it on a post-it note and steered Sandy towards the door.

'We should wait here.'

'No, we should leave and come back later.' Jake was adamant.

'It's wasting time.'

He held the door open and once in the street, she tugged her arm away. 'Let go! I could've persuaded her if you'd let me. What are we going to do now?'

Jake studied his phone, enlarging the screen. 'We are going to go to Jonjo's place because I have the address.' He held out his phone showing a photo of the screen and Jonjo's details.

'Oh.'

'Yeah, exactly. While you were offering pointless collateral, I was doing something.'

'OK, Mr Bond! The address?' Jake rattled it off and Sandy googled it. 'It's this way. I think,' she said, studying her phone and turning from left to right trying to orientate herself.

'Prospect Park is that direction.' Jake pointed behind him. 'Can you see it?'

'OK. We need to go this way.' Sandy waved them ahead with her phone and began walking.

'Are you sure?'

'I know how to read a map.'

'Just checking.'

Sandy ignored him and they walked on.

CHAPTER 10

The blue light was throbbing on Sandy's phone, showing they were going in the right direction. They crossed Flatbush and reached Church Avenue, a massive fruit and veg shop spilling its wares onto the pavement next to a small deli. Sandy zoomed into the map as she took a left turn. 'Not much further.' She pointed to an apartment block in the distance and they walked into a quieter street arriving at the building entrance. 'Must be in here.'

Jake led the way. 'Lift's out of order.' They headed for the stairs and five floors later, out of breath, he knocked on the door of 521. They could hear a commotion going on inside, a shout followed by a short scream. He banged more loudly this time. 'Are you alright in there?'

Another wail. 'Help!'

'Let us in and we'll help you!'

The sound of furniture crashing over was followed by a thump on the door from the other side.

'Should I kick the door in?' Jake asked. He retreated ready to charge. 'Make way!' he shouted, sounding like a medieval knight. 'I'm coming in.' Sandy stopped him as the door opened slowly revealing a young woman, heavily pregnant.

'Can I help you?' Sandy moved towards her.

'My waters broke. It's coming! It's my second baba and it's coming right this minute!' Even through the strong Brooklyn accent Sandy understood the situation immediately. The woman doubled over and yelled as another contraction wracked her body. The door swung open wide as she lurched away.

Sandy entered and helped balance her. 'Have you called an ambulance?'

'No, I dropped my cell and couldn't bend to get it. Aaaaaaaaaargh!' The woman's face contorted with agony. 'It's coming!'

'Where's the bedroom?' The expectant mother nodded forward and Sandy supported her as best she could through the flat.

Jake was running in circles, hands in his hair. 'She's having a baby! She's having a baby!'

'Jake! Stop panicking. Phone an ambulance.'

'OK. Good. I'm on it.'

In the bedroom, Sandy held on to the woman as she stripped the quilt and top sheet back, then helped her on to the bed. 'When are you due?'

The woman lay her head on the pillows and clasped her beaded braids with both hands, a small wail coming out. 'Three weeks. Oh my god. It's coming. Eeeeegh!' The long shriek ended abruptly and was replaced with panting. 'Shit!'

'Where's the bathroom?' Sandy asked.

'Can't you hold on?'

'Washing my hands.' Sandy followed the raised finger and was back in a flash as Jake came in.

'Ambulance is on its way.'

'Jake, can you find some towels? Sheets, anything. And boil a kettle.' He left the room and Sandy gently asked the mother-to-be, 'What's your name?'

'Keisha. Aaaaargh!' she panted some more. 'This is crazy - who are you?'

Sandy busied herself pulling the top sheet over the woman and folding it back to create a tent. 'I'm Sandy, and we came to see Jonjo. Please don't worry, I was a midwife for over twenty years in Scotland.' She was trying to make the woman comfortable, removing her skirt and underwear. Her confident air meant Keisha complied, allowing Sandy to get her ready for the baby. 'I've delivered hundreds of babies. Hundreds!' She smiled at the mother-to-be. 'So although we've just met, we can do this together.'

Keisha smiled uncertainly before her body was wracked with another spasm.

'Remember your breathing techniques. I'm going to examine you now.'

'Owww! Here we go.' The woman clenched the sides of the bed and writhed in agony.

'Take deep breaths, you've done it before, you can do it again.' She guided the patient into rhythmic breathing, and Keisha watched her, taking strength from her experienced demeanour.

Jake returned, immediately averted his eyes, and walked blindly towards Sandy, holding out an assortment of linens. She placed them around and under Keisha as Jake leaned towards her and whispered in her ear. 'Umm, I thought you said you were an academic. Are you sure you can do this?'

'I was a midwife before I joined academia.' She turned to Keisha. 'Sweetheart, can Jake help you? He's a friend. Jake, could you hold the lady's hand if she needs it?'

Keisha gratefully took Jake's hand, squeezing so tightly he winced and opened his mouth to complain. Sandy shot a warning glance, silencing him immediately.

'Use this cloth to cool her brow, and keep the pillows propped up.' He gingerly mopped away at Keisha's forehead.

'OK. Keisha. Let's bring your baby into the world.' She pushed the pregnant woman's legs apart and got close. 'It's on its way. You're crowning perfectly. Are you ready to push?'

Jake clenched his teeth while Keisha wailed again and clamped harder on his hand.

'That's it. Let it out.' Between them, the birth got underway. Keisha breathed and pushed and Sandy encouraged and massaged her tummy. Jake kept her forehead cool and plumped the cushions with his free hand. With a final push, the baby slid out into Sandy's arms.

'It's a girl! A delightful baby girl. Let me clear her airways. Keisha, you've been amazing. Jake, can you bring in a basin of warm water please.'

Jake was staring at the baby, tears in his eyes, still holding on to Keisha's hand.

'Jake,' Sandy said gently.

'Yes, yes, of course.' He left the room.

Sandy attended to the baby and then a beautiful cry rang out into the room.

'Here she comes, baby wants to be with Mum.' As she held the baby in one arm, Sandy helped Keisha undo her blouse and laid the baby across her mother's chest. She took a small towel and placed it over the baby's head and body. 'To keep her warm.'

Keisha was crying as she blessed her daughter and caressed her tiny face. Sandy gently covered the mother's front with a clean sheet as Jake came back. They could hear a siren outside.

'Jake,' Sandy whispered, 'can you leave us alone for a moment, while I get Keisha sorted?' He placed the basin on the bedside table and quietly left the room. Sandy took two metal clasps out of her hair and clamped the cord. 'It's make-shift. It'll do until the paramedics get here, and they'll deal with everything. Let's get you a bit more comfortable.'

Gently, she wiped the baby who was heralding her arrival in the world with her tiny lungs as she nestled into Keisha's chest. Sandy washed and dried the new mum's face too.

Suddenly there was a disturbance in the hallway. 'Who the hell are you? If you don't get outta here I'm calling the police!' a woman shouted.

'Etta!' Keisha called, 'I'm in here.'

A woman bearing a close resemblance to Keisha dashed into the bedroom. 'Keisha! What's going on?'

'It's fine. They delivered the baby.'

'You've had the baby?' She came over to the bed and Sandy retreated. 'Oh my Gawd! Boy or girl?'

'It's a girl.'

'Aww. A sister for Luis. She's so cute!' she drawled. 'But hold on! Who are you two? Who's the hairy guy in the skirt?'

Before Sandy could answer, two paramedics arrived. They quickly assessed the situation, quietly asking Keisha questions before taking out their instruments and cutting the cord and attending to the new mother. Etta held Keisha's hand while she was treated and Jake hung about the doorway, watching what was going on. He took out a handkerchief and blew his nose, still visibly moved by what had happened.

'Did you deliver?' one of the paramedics asked.

Sandy nodded. 'I used to be a midwife.'

'There's no used to about it. She's a lucky new mom to have had you.'

'How did you get here? How come you're with ma sis?' Etta asked.

'I'm Sandy. We came to get our passports from Jon-jo, I'd left them in the car and we arrived at the same time your sister's waters broke.'

'Wow. Miraculous, you arriving just in time.'

'Does Jonjo live here too?'

'Yeah, he's my husband,' said Etta.

The paramedics gently lifted her sister, clutching her baby daughter, onto a gurney.

'Keisha took Sandy's hand as she was wheeled past. 'Thank you. I don't know how things would've turned out without you.'

Sandy clasped the hand in her own. 'I'm glad I was here and could help. Take care.' The mother had tears in her eyes as she was wheeled away by the paramedics.

'Let me get the doors for you.' Jake followed them.

Keisha yelled out, 'Etta, call Adio. And bring my cell. It's under the dresser.' A few seconds later came a faint, 'God bless you Sandy!' from the stairwell.

Etta was smiling but still in shock. 'I can't believe she's had the baby. And who's the hairy guy? Is he your man?'

'No! That's Jake. His passport was left in the car too.'

'Jonjo's at the barbers. Did you go to the depot? Did Bill tell you to come here?'

'Not exactly. Cheryl—'

Jake came in even more out of breath than before and panted out, 'You were incredible. The whole thing was incredible.'

'Oh my God,' Etta exclaimed. 'Your outfit!'

Sandy looked and saw her blazer, trousers and cream shirt were covered in baby gunk and blood.

'Oh Lordy, you have to get these off. Go to the bathroom while I find some clothes.'

As Sandy left, she saw Jake sink on a chair, still dazed. In the bathroom, she peeled her soiled clothes off and folded them as best she could, her hands shaking. Her reflection in the mirror told her baby gunk was in her hair too. Etta knocked and came in.

'Use the shower and help yourself to any products. Here's a towel – the last one.' Etta took Sandy's hand and held it to her. 'God bless you, Sandy, for being here. You never know how these things can go down.' Etta had tears in her eyes as she drew Sandy into a hug. 'Thank you' she whispered. 'Damn, I'd better go and call the poppa.'

When Sandy returned to the bedroom, she looked like a different woman. Etta had lent her jeans, tie-dyed T-shirt and a shocking-pink bejewelled leather jacket. The clothes swamped her lean frame and she'd pulled the jeans belt to the last notch to keep them from slipping over her slim hips. Her hair was damp after the shower and her trembling hands had broken the last hair clip, leaving it to curl naturally around her face and shoulders. She could sense Jake's eyes on her.

'Thanks for these, I'll make sure I bring them back.'

'Don't worry about the jeans, they're Keisha's and it'll be a while before she gits her ass in them again!' Etta smiled. 'But I love my bling-bling jacket.'

'Where will we find Jonjo?' Jake asked and Etta gave them directions.

'It's near the car depot, you'll have passed the barber-shop on the way. I'll tell him you're coming. But I need to get off to the hospital.' After saying their farewells, Sandy and Jake left.

CHAPTER 11

Sandy fiddled with the belt of the jeans. It was odd and uncomfortable wearing a stranger's clothes. Jake walked backwards in front of Sandy. 'You delivered a baby! I've never seen anything like it.' He stopped while she walked towards him. 'It was awesome! That is a real talent. You never said you were a midwife.'

'I haven't been for a while. I lecture on midwifery now.'

Jake turned full circle. 'It was unbelievable.' He walked on and despite his exuberance, Sandy stopped and doubled over. There was an ache in the pit of her stomach and she drew in deep breaths to steady the emotion rising inside. Jake was oblivious, continuing to wax lyrical about the miracle of birth as he walked. Slowly, she managed to gather herself and, her body still trembling, continued while he waited for her.

'I'm sorry, you must be so used to it while I'm banging on about miracles.'

'I'm fine. Let's just get the passports.' Sandy moved off and Jake got into step beside her as they crossed onto Flatbush Avenue towards the depot. With a few twists and turns they stood outside a traditional barbershop with the red, blue and white striped pole on one side and artistic representations of tattoos in the other window. A huge picture of a smiling Etta at work with a tattoo pen towered over them. Sandy stepped inside and was immediately taken by Jonjo into a full-bodied hug.

'Thank you! Ya see – things happen for a reason. You left your passports and I forgot to hand them in – just so you could deliver Keisha's baba. It's a miracle you were there.' He clapped Jake's back. 'And I guess if you weren't loaded, it would never have happened either!'

Jake was sheepish as Jonjo handed him the passports.

'How can I thank you? I don't do the ladies, sorry Sandy. Jake, how long has it been, man? I mean, you need some serious cutting action – the beard and the hair – it's a crusty vibe. Let me do you.'

Jake regarded his long beard in the mirror. 'Years. It's been years.' He ran a hand through his hair. 'This has to come off some time, I suppose. Etta shrieked when she saw me.'

'You can't be frightening the ladies.' Before he had a chance to refuse, Jonjo wrestled Jake's jacket off and settled him in a chair.

'Do you mind waiting?' Jake asked Sandy.

'No.' She retreated to a window seat.

'Take off the sweater, the neck's too high for the shave.'

'It'll be fine,' said Jake. 'I'll hold it out of your way.'

'C'mon, take it off. Let me do my job. You must be cookin' in that big woolly thing.'

Reluctantly, Jake removed the ancient Aran jumper over his head, his top riding up with it, revealing a hairy chest and a snake of soft fuzz cut off by the kilt. He pulled the T-shirt firmly over his belly.

'Are you wearing a Brig tee?' Sandy asked to take her mind off the exposure of his chest, and more. The Brig World Tour 2004 was emblazoned across the front, the list of cities hidden under Jake's folded arms. It was tight across his chest and biceps; a ripped side seam gave room for his stomach and Jake was squirming at being caught wearing a promo shirt for his own band.

'And why not? It was our first international tour.'

'The Brig? "Goodbye!" Did you used to be in that band?' Jonjo brushed out Jake's long hair as he began a tortuous rendition of their biggest hit. Thankfully, it didn't last as he ran out of lyrics.

Sandy was aware it had been a long time since The Brig had played or released a record. Once she'd met Mike, she didn't follow them as she had before. She took in Jake's powerful biceps and could see a tattoo on his forearm. 'Zaraya' entwined around flowers and a traditional heart. Jake crossed his arms the other way, hiding the tattoo from view and was saved by Jonjo throwing a gown over him. Zaraya. Of course. He'd married the backing singer. She shivered. It was uncomfortable knowing about Jake's private life. Her knowledge gleaned from gossip magazines and she was ashamed of her once avid desire to know everything she could about him.

'I'm going out for a wander. How long will you be, Jonjo?'

'Gimme an hour. This is gonna take some time.'

Outside a delicious aroma escaping from a nearby restaurant tickled Sandy's nostrils. She mooched past a small parade of shops, with its nail bars, hairdressers and delis – but no boutiques where she might buy replacement clothes. Her carefully worked out plans were in tatters - Tick Tocks, the Statue of Liberty, Ellis Island Ferry – all missed – and there was no way Battery Park was going to happen. They could stay on the bucket list for a return trip with Mike. But she would make the Grand Central Station tour and although she'd cancelled the Oyster Bar, she could find somewhere else. Her schedule was not all lost. Pleased with having a plan for later she made her way to one of the delis and bought a coffee, taking it outside to a little bench by the window. Sitting in the April sunshine she watched the world go by: delivery trucks and joggers, fast cars with loud music, dog walkers wrangling five or six dogs apiece, and women studying their newly painted nails as they left the salon across the road. Sandy pondered why she and Mike had never embraced café society on their many trips to Europe. They would always move on quickly; any time spent not seeing a famous landmark or museum was considered time wasted. She found she was enjoying the opportunity to sit and watch the constant stream of passers-by. This was the only time she'd ever been alone in a strange city. Holidays with Isobel, followed by trips with Mike, ensured she'd never been solitary. Daydreams of driving from New York to LA, had stayed only daydreams. Being here, on her own, in this moment, made her feel alive and hopeful, different from the bored housewife she'd become. She contemplated the size of the US and how easy it would be to get lost in it. To take off and drive for days before hitting the west coast. Was Jake right when he said holding on to a schedule kept her safe and secure? His disdain had rankled, mostly because there was more than a grain of truth in his insight.

As she sipped the strong coffee, she tried to process the events of the afternoon. She'd delivered a baby! She hadn't held a baby since... She stood abruptly, tossing the remains of her drink into a nearby bin.

On the hour precisely she opened the door into the barbershop and there was Jake Cabrelli – a much more recognisable version. He was cleanshaven and his long hair was cut into a short textured style, following the natural wave of his hair. Surprisingly, there was still quite a bit of black in with the grey and it brought out the blue of his eyes. Awkwardness surged in her as she confronted this vision from her past. She blushed intensely, feeling a sudden shyness toward him.

Jake was staring at himself in the mirror, unsure of the reflection. 'What do you think?' he asked her.

'I think you need some decent clothes to complete the transformation.'

'I guess I do, considering my luggage will still be going round the carousel at Newark.'

They added his jumper to Sandy's clothes bag and after a lot of hugging and handshaking with Jonjo, managed to hail a cab back to Manhattan.

'I haven't bought clothes in years. I don't even know where to go anymore in this city.'

'Have you got money?'

'Yeah!' He sounded offended. 'Of course I do.'

'Keep your hair on. I meant to spend on decent clothes.'

'I'm no stingbum.'

Sandy rolled her eyes. 'If you've plenty of money you should go to Bloomingdale's and get a personal shopper.'

'A personal shopper?'

'Yup. They take your size, ask about your style, and bring a selection of clothes to try on. It doesn't even cost anything and saves you wading through racks of stuff.'

'I thought you hadn't been here before.'

'I can read a shopping guide.'

Jake leaned forward in the taxi. 'Driver. Can you take us to Bloomingdale's please?'

'Then can you take me on to the City Hotel East 34th at Lexington please?'

'You're not coming?'

'I've got time to go to the hotel for fresh clothes and do the tour I've booked at Grand Central. I can leave your guitar at reception.'

'Ah yes. Your *schedule*.'

'You don't need to say it like that. My *schedule*,' Sandy mimicked.

'You'd think after today's experience you'd have learned the best way to see a city is to go with the flow. Look what happened today!'

'Exactly why I like a schedule. Nothing untoward. Nothing unpredictable.' She held Etta's jacket open. 'Look at me. I'm wearing a neon pink jacket too big for me, Keisha's jeans and Etta's T-shirt, my hair's all over the place and I can't even remember where I'm supposed to be.' She took out her schedule and studied it.

Jake whipped it from her hand. 'You're supposed to be at Battery Park.' He scanned the plans for Thursday and snorted. 'Every hour accounted for, including how long you spend in the shower.' Sandy made a grab for it but he lowered the window and tossed it out.

'I have another copy anyway.'

'Why am I not surprised? What's up with you? You were fine a minute ago.'

She bit her lip, not trusting herself to speak.

'Sandy?'

'I haven't delivered a baby since ... in a long time. It kind of gets to you.' She blew her nose. Jake was immediately regretful.

'I'm sorry. And I'm sorry I threw your schedule away.'

She edged away from him and used her compact mirror to apply lipstick as best she could in the bouncing taxi.

'Please come with me,' he said. 'I'm a blockhead. Blockhead is mid-seventeenth century by the way and comes from the name for a hat-maker's wooden shape.'

Sandy smiled, despite herself.

'I haven't bought anything for ages,' he said. 'I've no idea about fashion anymore. Please help me?'

The 'please help me' reminded Sandy of the anguished 'Please help me' on the plane.

'I'm supposed to be at Bloomingdale's tomorrow.' She paused. 'It's possible I could fit something else in.'

'So, the precious schedule can be rearranged, eh?'

'Don't push it.'

Jake laughed and told the driver they would get out at Bloomingdale's.

'On Broadway?' the driver asked.

Jake raised a questioning brow at Sandy. 'Yes. On Broadway. The other one's away up near Central Park.'

'I promise I'll bring you back to the hotel after, get my guitar and you can resume normal service.'

CHAPTER 12

Sandy's heart fluttered when she went inside, the department store was so famous and her head was spinning as she tried to take it in. Bright lights highlighted the various fashion brands. Expensively dressed shoppers browsed, tempting displays everywhere. She inhaled the strong smell of leather as they walked through the handbag department.

'Personal shopper, fourth floor.' Jake pointed towards a sign and charged ahead, Sandy running behind as he strode up the escalators, his kilt swinging away in front of her, flashing his thighs. It would be such fun when she told Isobel how she had spent her day - with Jake Cabrelli. Since the haircut he was no longer a dodgy middle-aged man who resembled a vagrant, and it was difficult to recalibrate without slipping into being the fan she once was. She and Isobel would go to the concert on Saturday night and see The Brig on stage, her brief encounter with celebrity over. Although he didn't seem like an idol anymore – more like an ordinary slightly troubled guy who was a bit lost. Was Jonjo right? Maybe things did happen for a reason – Mike having to work, Isobel's virtual lover deciding to meet in real life, Jake taking the slimming pills and getting drunk. It had all brought her to Keisha's door at the exact moment she needed help.

'The desk's over there.' When they reached it Jake pushed Sandy in front.

'Hello Madame. I'm Camille, one of the personal shoppers for today. How can I help you?'

Sandy could see Camille, with her exaggerated European accent, was eyeing Etta's jacket and the fashion choices of her companion.

'My friend here needs some clothes. Enough for – how long?'

Jake tugged his T-shirt over his paunch so the soft dark hairs Sandy was too aware of were hidden.

'Just the weekend.'

Camille cast an experienced eye over Jake. 'Monsieur. Oui, I can help with that – and get rid of this ancient thing... Kilt, skirt, whatever you might call it. We had a last-minute cancellation, otherwise... Please fill in this form, give me size details.' She waggled a finger. 'And no little lies.' Camille confided to Sandy, 'Men are the worst and it wastes so much of the time.'

Sandy was drifting off wondering if Jake would be on her return flight if he was only here for the weekend.

'You can sit. Sit. Sit there.' She waved them off imperiously towards a large lip-shaped couch.

They sat on the opulent red velvet furniture and Jake filled in the form. Realising Sandy was nosing over his shoulder, he hid his writing, schoolboy style. She smiled and averted her eyes.

'What do I need? Jeans? I've no idea about my style, even if I ever had one.'

'Old rocker style?'

'Haha.'

'Shirts? T-shirts? Jumper. You can't keep wearing that ancient Aran thing. Boots?' She indicated his battered ones.

'No! These are fine.'

'I don't want to be talking out of turn here, but my guess is you were taking those slimming pills because you want to be a version of your former self. Or at least like a rock star after you've been in exile living like a hermit.'

'Well...'

'You're already halfway there with the haircut and shave. The size you are doesn't matter as long as you wear clothes that suit you and fit properly.'

'You sound like a magazine.'

'Do you want to be yesterday's man or not?'

'You are harsh.'

'Jake?'

'I want to look like I've been living a life since we split.'

'So, shirts – black and navy? Jeans, tops, the boots, you'll also need underwear. Socks.'

Jake added to the list as Camille came over and took it from him.

'OK, Mr Brig.'

Sandy glanced at him and raised her eyebrows.

He shrugged. 'Umm, I'm not sure I know my size anymore. I've been wearing a kilt for a while.'

'Stand up and let me see.'

Jake did so, uncomfortable under Camille's scrutiny.

'OK. I see. Give me half an hour and I'll bring a selection for you to try. To save time, you might want to go to the gents' department on the floor below and choose your own personal wear?' She trotted off in her high heels with the list.

'I'll mooch around here while you get your smalls. I'm sure you don't need help with those,' Sandy said but before she could begin her mooch, a text pinged in from Mike.

All OK? Haven't heard from you? Going to bed here. Miss you. xxx

She quickly texted, *I miss you too but we've had a great day*. She didn't tell him she'd been on her own. Not even on her own - with a strange man. She added, *Going for dinner soon. Love you. xxx*

Then she texted Isobel to check she hadn't been murdered by a Texan psychopath. *How's your Romeo? Have you had a good day? x*

Isobel sent a string of suggestive emojis. *Getting dressed to go out for a quick bite. How's your day been? Happy on your own? x*

Sandy's fingers hovered over the screen, considering how much to say. *All good. Had a fab day. Will text later about tomorrow. Have fun! x*

She wandered over to the clothes rails but stopped when she caught her reflection in a mirror. *Gawd, pink is awful on me*. She posed and moved with the jacket, liking the shape – such a contrast from her blazers and suits. The jeans were fine apart from the size. She noticed her beige sensible walking shoes poking out and saw how ridiculous they were with the jeans. Drifting further she came across a selection of women's leather jackets. They were so soft and tactile to the touch, and she admired the exquisite quality and finish. Removing Etta's bling-bling, she tried on a black leather and posed in front of the mirror. It was biker style, with nickel fittings, lots of zips. It moulded to her body and gave her shape, emphasising her trim waist by flicking out at the hips. It was luxurious and daring, a complete contrast from her usual choices. She glanced at the price tag. Perhaps not. Mike would have a fit. Sandy returned the jacket to its hanger.

Jake stood behind her. 'You should buy it.'

'It's not my kind of thing.'

'You want it. You should get it. Thought you were a footloose and fancy-free type person who does anything they please?'

Camille came towards them, dragging a rail behind her. 'Oui, madame, you did suit that jacket. Better than the pink and I can get the rest of your outfit for you. You need boots, these shoes are...' The personal shopper scrunched her nose. Jake laughed. 'And you, Mr Brig, you are old rocker man, no?' It was Sandy's turn to snigger.

'So I have brought you the dark colours mixed with some brights for the eyes. Shall we go through?'

Jake gave Sandy a mock fearful gurn as he followed Camille into the changing rooms. He allowed himself to be ushered into a large, curtained area, with surrounding mirrors and a luxurious chaise longue. Camille brought in the clothes rail and faced him. Jake watched her, unsure of the procedure.

'Let me have the jacket.'

He peeled it off and handed it to her.

'And the rest.'

'Are you going to watch me?'

'Monsieur! Not watch, but this is my job, I help the customer.'

'I'm fine, I can dress myself.' He was mortified at the idea of removing his clothes in front of her.

Camille eyed her customer. 'OK.' She selected two pairs of jeans and placed them on the chaise longue with the jacket. 'I have given you two sizes, try both.'

She left, and Jake made sure the curtain was closed properly behind her, peering out to check there was no-one else around. He removed his boots, and untied the kilt, letting it fall to the ground, the T-shirt followed. Jake braced himself to peek at his 300-degree image. He clutched his belly and jiggled it. Ugh. He had a concert in two days. Why hadn't he been able to lose weight? He was going to look like some gross ancient has-been on stage. He felt sick with nerves. Whipping the fisherman's socks off, he threw them in the corner and checking the sizes, he opted for the larger jeans and put them on.

They were too big! He happily tried the smaller size and with a deep breath held his stomach in and zipped them up. He needed the larger version of the shirt and once it was on and buttoned, he looked in the mirror. He couldn't see any muffin top from the jeans, it actually wasn't too bad.

Camille's voice came from outside the curtain. 'Hello, how are things, Monsieur? Can I come in?'

'I'm decent,' he said.

She whipped back the curtain. 'Ah oui. The smaller size, yes?' Before Jake could react she had her fingers in his waistband and was checking the fit. She followed this by going behind him and spreading her hands across his shoulders. 'The larger. Superb. OK, I'll get more options. Jake could see himself from all sides in the mirror. He hated to admit it, but Sandy was right, the clothes made a difference.

Sandy was sitting outside the dressing rooms when Jake came out in bare feet with black jeans and long-sleeved black shirt. Wow. His blue eyes sparkled, and he still had the longest lashes. She remembered how much she'd envied them in the past. She gave it a thumbs up.

'I still don't understand how my feet got hurt,' he said.

She was horrified to see dark bruising across the bridge of each foot. She looked away, reddening at how she'd stamped on his feet to waken him up. 'I've no idea. Did you fall at some point?'

'I don't remember.' He disappeared into the changing room and was soon out again wearing dark denim jeans and navy shirt. Another thumbs up from Sandy. This time he did a 360-degree turn.

'Yeah, yeah,' she said. 'You're not on the catwalk, you know.'

'I was feeling it. You were right – it is an improvement on the jumper and kilt combo.'

'Told you so.'

'Clever clogs.'

Camille went past with more clothing. A moment later Jake was out again with the same jeans and a black cap-sleeved T-shirt. Ooft. He looked good in that. Sandy liked the way it was tight across his chest and showed off his powerful biceps. She blushed again, and not because of guilt this time. Not usually a fan of tattoos, she liked seeing his forearm muscles moving under it, even if it did say Zaraya.

'Well, my fashion guru – any good?' Sandy was plucked out of her fantasy.

'It's OK.'

'Just OK? No thumbs up?'

She gave him one.

Boots, sweaters and more shirts came out for the thumbs up or occasionally, a thumbs down.

Camille arrived with more clothing and invited Sandy to a changing area. 'Here you are. You need a different style too.' She had selected navy denim jeans, black boots with a Cuban heel and a simple black crew top.

Sandy loved the whole outfit, enjoying the casual style of the denim and boots. She tried on the leather jacket and could see a resemblance to the young person she'd seen in the photos before she'd left home – youthful, unrestrained – connecting with a part of herself she feared she might have lost. Who cares if Mike baulked at the cost? It was her money she was spending. Grateful to Camille for her help and before she allowed any doubts, she crunched her credit card at the desk and waited for Jake.

At last, he was at the counter beside her in denim jeans, boots and sporting the hot cap-sleeved top, surrounded by shopping bags. Sandy's heartbeat was rising and she had to step away while he paid for his shopping. There was a confidence radiating from him, a different man from this morning. Was it only this morning they'd got off the flight? They headed for the exit.

'I've got an idea. Why don't we buy something for the baby and take it to Jonjo's house? We can return the borrowed clothes to Etta at the same time. Dump this bag at the hotel.' He looked at Sandy. 'I remember your schedule for today, and you'd already put a black cross against the Oyster Bar, so tonight you're free. I'll treat you to dinner to thank you – and so endeth the maddest day in New York both of us will ever have. How does that sound?'

She stepped off the escalator.

'Look! Baby clothes. C'mon, it'll be fun.' His excitement was infectious but Sandy dithered. It was one thing when he was channelling Gandalf but he'd morphed into something else. She was married. But Mike was in Dundee. No-one would ever know, it's not like they were doing anything. It was a lovely idea to go with a gift and she did have to return the pink jacket.

'Isn't it late to go visiting? By the time we get there—'

'This is the city that never sleeps, it's never too late for anything.'

Sandy gave in. 'OK. But no pink and you choose.'

'No pink.'

Jake bought a hideously expensive designer sleepsuit in rainbow colours and, back outside, they hailed another cab. The day had taken on a bewildering quality heightened by lack of sleep and jet lag and Sandy was drawn in by Jake's ebullience.

'I haven't had this much fun in years. Retail therapy is a thing!' he said.

Another taxi ride had them at the City Hotel. Sandy pulled her suit and blouse out of the bag. They were in too much of a state to hand in for cleaning; anyone would suspect murder. She squashed them back into the bag and put it all in the bin. Everything else went with her into the bathroom. She washed and applied fresh make-up. Out of habit she lifted her hair, ready to fix the curls away from her face. Instead, she stopped and let it fall naturally. The leather jacket went on and she stared at the stranger in the mirror.

'What do you think?' She came into the room and posed in front of Jake who couldn't hide the approval in his eyes.

'Well?'

'Glad you got rid of those ridiculous shoes; I swear my mum had the same pair.' He got up and moved towards the bathroom.

'Is that all you can say?'

He paused. 'Positively pulchritudinous,' he said and closed the door behind him.

What does that mean? She knew she'd been insulted and whipped out her phone, stabbing out p u l c r i.. what? 'Pulchritudinous' popped up on Google – 'beautiful'. Her heart swelled in her chest – he thought she was beautiful. Flustered she busied herself with storing her handbag contents in her leather jacket as Jake returned.

'OK. Here's the baby gift.' He lifted a bag. 'I'll leave my stuff here. I'll bring you home after we've delivered the gift and had dinner, then I'll head off to my hotel. Does this plan work for you?'

'Let's eat before we go. I'm starving!' She folded Etta's clothes into the bag.

'There used to be one of the best Mexican restaurants near here. They did the meanest margaritas and tacos to die for. Shall we see if it's still open?'

'Only if it can be my treat – you've paid for all the taxis today.'

'The margaritas are on you. Let's go.'

CHAPTER 13

When Sandy walked out onto 34th Street with Jake, it was as if someone else inhabited her body. She caught a glimpse in a shop window as they walked past – a cool couple going out for the night. Mike would be sleeping soundly at home, completely unaware his wife was out on the town with a rock star, or an ex-rock star. Did Mike find her beautiful after all this time? She'd no idea.

'It's here.' Jake darted down a set of steep stairs beside a neon sign flashing 'Franks'. They entered a busy restaurant, humming with conversation and buzzing with waiters flourishing large trays of food. They were escorted to a private booth with old fashioned candle lights attached to the wall. The waiter placed menus in front of them.

'Do you still do the taster menu?'

'Yes, sir, we do.'

'The taster's great, a whole load of tiny dishes and if you like something you order the full portion.'

'Great.' Sandy would never allow Mike to choose for her but as she was channelling an unidentified persona tonight, she would go with the flow.

'And two classic margaritas. You do like margaritas, don't you?'

'Yes. But don't make mine strong, please.'

'No problem.' The waiter gathered the menus and left the table.

Billy Joel's New York State of Mind was playing out. 'Doesn't sound very Mexican?'

'Nah, they favour tracks and acts related to the city.'

The cocktails appeared. 'Here's mud in your eye!' Jake clinked Sandy's glass. It was chilled, tangy and fresh and went straight to her head.

'I wonder where that saying comes from,' Sandy mused.

'It's from the 1890s, it's a toast to self because if there's mud in your eye it means my horse is in front and kicking mud in the air from the race.'

'Are you a walking dictionary?'

'Sometimes there's too much time in the world.'

The food arrived and Jake told her about the variety of dishes. More drinks appeared and Sandy hadn't even heard him ordering.

'Oh, you don't need to ask, they bring fresh when they see it's finished. You've got to tell them to stop.'

'Stop! Two is my limit.'

'This has to be a three-margarita night.'

They spoke about the day, going over it from the moment her hair was caught by the guitar – and because Jake didn't remember it, Sandy obligingly regaled him with an embellished tale of how she'd managed to get him out of the airport and into a car. Jake took it in good part and they relaxed, comfortable with each other.

'Why did you hide yourself away?'

Jake played with the stem of his glass. 'I was married to Zaraya. She used to be part of The Brig as a backing singer.'

'I remember her. A phenomenal voice.'

'It is indeed. Well, we were on tour in the States and I found out she'd been unfaithful. With Iain.' Jake rubbed away at an imaginary spot on the palm of his hand. 'Turned out the other guys knew. I found out minutes before going on stage when I saw them kissing. I only managed three numbers of the show. Then I lost the plot, tried to land one on Iain and got Stu instead, kicked out and hit Danny, who was bashing his sticks on Iain's head. It turned into a huge rammy with bouncers hauling us apart, one of them inadvertently breaking my nose. I was gushing blood over my shirt and walked off. Got a car to the airport, and the press did too. They were on the flight, and even more of them were there when I got off at the other side, shouting and taking photos. It was in all the papers with pictures of the 'The Brig Brawl' or the fracas, the melee, rumpus – they all had different names for it – a square go, fisticuffs – depending on the paper. They even followed me to my Dad's in Dundee and camped outside so I had to leave.' Jake shook his head. 'When humiliation is so public, it's like your insides have been scraped out. I found my cottage in Angus and stayed.'

'It must have been horrible.' Sandy vaguely remembered seeing it in the press. Her focus had been elsewhere, no longer following what the band did.

'The whole fame, celebrity thing – it's brilliant for selling records, and in the early days it was great fun, we loved it. The other side is hellish. When Stu appeared last year, we went to a pub. Of course, someone took photos of him, and although they didn't recognise me because I was such a state, I became a meme on social media, arse hanging out my kilt while I puked outside.' Jake gave a wry smile. 'They upskirted me and the papers gave Stu a tough time for hanging out with a vagrant. I became a punchline to a joke about drunk Scottish men.'

'I did see that. How awful.'

'Never leave home without your pants. At least I wasn't identified. I don't even need to leave home, I have my recording studio, my instruments, everything I need.'

'So why now? Why come back now?'

'I guess because Stu can be very persuasive. He's often mooted the possibility of getting us together, and when he came over last year, he told me Danny had been struggling. It had been easy for him and Iain getting work, but not so much for Danny. Stu's my oldest friend, and the four of us have been together since school. I thought enough time had passed. I'm not so sure now that I'm here.' Jake concentrated on the rest of his margarita, shaking his head at the memories. 'But hey, as Jonjo says, maybe it was meant to be. I still can't get over the baby. It was mind-blowing. I never imagined I'd be part of something so ... life affirming. You must have delivered loads. Why did you stop? It's the one job for life – that and funeral directors!' Jake was amused by his own joke. 'I mean, why would you stop doing something so awe-inspiring?'

Sandy neatened the cutlery on the table, unsure what to say. She opened her mouth to speak and nothing came out. She swallowed instead. Moments passed. 'The truth?' She fiddled with the condiments, neatening them up. 'I really wanted a baby of my own, but it never happened. Horrible miscarriages and rounds of IVF and by then I was in my forties. I thought it was too late but miraculously I got pregnant and carried the baby much longer than the others. But at twenty-two weeks I went into labour.' She lifted her glass and realised her hand was shaking. Gently, Jake took it from her and placed it back on the table. 'She only lived a few hours. I couldn't bear my job after that.' Her head swam, she must be drunk, she'd only ever spoken to Isobel about it. And, she realised, she'd cut Mike entirely from the story. When Jake placed his hand on top of hers, she withdrew it, and zipped her jacket to the top, suddenly feeling naked and exposed. She shook her head. 'Too much information.'

There was a long pause, then Jake said softly, 'I'm so sorry for your loss. Sorry you went through such sadness.'

'*C'est la vie.*' She picked up her glass again, her hand gripping it tightly. She raised it to Jake and took a gulp of cocktail to hide the sob burbling in her throat. The waiter placed two more margaritas on the table.

Sandy eyed the fresh cocktail with trepidation. 'I guess this is a four-margarita night.'

'I hope I don't have to carry you to the hotel this time.' Jake's remark lightened the mood. By the time the bill came another margarita later, Sandy couldn't stop laughing as she searched through the pockets in the jacket, finding her card in the last one.

'I do love this jacket. I don't feel like me in it. It's a magic jacket.'

'It suits you. No more suits.'

'I like suits too!'

They giggled their way out of the restaurant. Sandy tripped on the bottom step and Jake took her hand, helped her the rest of the way. When she flung out a hand like an actor in a movie, amazingly, a taxi screeched to a halt. 'It's the magic New York jacket,' she declared and they clambered into the back.

CHAPTER 14

The taxi tooted its way through the evening traffic. Sandy's head was whirring, it felt like a week had passed since she'd met Isobel at the airport. She watched the city flash by, enjoying the combination of strangeness and familiarity. More than 1.7 million people were living their lives on this island of Manhattan and she was one tiny speck in amongst them. But an individual speck, on her own, or at least not with Mike or Isobel. She stole a glance at Jake staring out the window at his side. He was a quite different man from the initially drunk and then pugnacious character she'd encountered that morning, with his own painful past that he'd been hiding from.

The bright lights of the Manhattan Bridge brought her out of her reverie as they crossed it for the third time that day and it wasn't long before they streamed off the other side and were on their way to their destination.

'Hey, Jonjo's place is still open. Can we stop here, please?' Jake said. The driver braked and they tumbled out, Sandy wavering slightly.

Loud music was blasting out of the barber shop and Jake steered Sandy to the entrance. 'They must be wetting the baby's head.'

He opened the door and Sandy stepped into a party in full swing. The entire neighbourhood appeared to be crowded into the shop, half of them dancing to the salsa beats coming from the speakers. In the midst of the action, Jonjo was skilfully using a cut-throat razer to shave a customer while a tattoo artist worked away on another client beside him.

'Heya.' Jonjo yelled as he spotted them through the crowd. 'Adio! Adio! This is Sandy – she delivered your baby.'

A young man holding a pitcher of a fruity mixture, danced over to them. 'Sandy!' Adio waltzed her around the room. 'Thank you. I am grateful to you, being there for Keisha.' He kissed her exuberantly on both cheeks.

'Jake has a gift, and I wanted to return Etta's clothes.'

Etta appeared through the throng. 'I was worried I'd never see my bling-bling again.' She put it on, wearing it with a style Sandy knew she herself would never have. 'Although I see you gotta sporty leather number of your own! Adio, this is Jake and he called the ambulance!' This got a cheer from the crowd and Jake bowed. Adio's default movement was the cha-cha and he danced to find a couple of glasses and danced back, filling them before handing them over. 'To Sandy and Jake! Thanks, guys, for being there.' The guests raised their glasses and cheered.

When the jug came round again, Sandy immediately held her glass out. 'This is delicious. What is it?'

'It's a pocheen we been cookin' up. A kind of punchy Sangria.'

The music pumped out and the crowd danced again. Sandy, inhibitions gone with the margaritas and sangria, joined in. As she danced, Jake showed her merengue steps, and she began moving with confidence. She was far away from the boredom and disappointments at home. She wanted to live for the moment and enjoy the celebrations for the life that had arrived today and she had been a part of. She danced and danced, lost in the music, not caring who was watching, until an over-exuberant spin took her out of the spell and she flopped onto one of the barber's chairs.

'Had enough Sandy?' someone asked.

'Need to rest my legs.' How long had they been going? It was forever ago they'd boarded the plane; so much had happened. Where was Jake? The dancing crowd parted slightly and she saw him sitting at a table with a man working on his tattoo.

Sandy tottered through. 'You're getting a tattoo?' She saw work had been done on 'Zaraya', eliminating the letters with flowering roses.

'It's time to move on. It's been that kind of day.'

'I want a tattoo!' Sandy exclaimed.

'Are you sure? You've had quite a few—'

'I desperately need a tattoo!'

The artist didn't take his eyes from his work: 'Etta! You gotta customer here.'

'Sandy, you really want a tattoo?' asked Jonjo as he came over. 'I tell ya, you are not the same person as the one who got into my car this morning.'

Etta placed a paper sheet on another tattoo bed. 'Are you sure, honey?'

'Yes. A small one.' She whipped her jacket off and bared her shoulder. 'Here. Carys. C-A-R-Y-S. Something simple and heavenly.'

Etta prepared her tools. 'An adorable name, honey, and I will make it perfect for you.'

Sandy was grateful Etta didn't ask any questions as she fired up her pen. It wasn't as sore as she'd imagined it would be, or maybe the drinks had anesthetised her. It was good to have Carys ingrained on her body, a tribute to a dearly-loved child who hadn't survived and who was never spoken of. She watched as the design evolved around the name. Instead of loss, shame and broken dreams, the tattoo would be a celebration of a daughter who would never be forgotten. Etta had drawn the name in a simple font and used daisies to intersperse the border. It was sweet and gentle, the yellows and pinks far removed from the more familiar darker inks.

Etta wrapped clingfilm around it. 'This needs to stay on for a couple of days – even in the shower – to keep it clean.'

Sandy slid from the bed. She found it difficult to speak and held Etta to her for a moment. She paid at the till while Jake's tattoo was being strapped. The barber shop had emptied.

'Jake still has to get his completed. I'm going to finish it off with some finer flowers. Six pm Sunday, Jake?'

'Good for me.'

Jonjo came over and poured them white rum shots. 'To the baba and new buddies.' Sandy tossed her drink back, shaking her head as she felt the hard spirit at the back of her throat. Supported by Jake, she floated out into a cool, fresh night. The roads were empty with only an occasional car driving past, no opportunity for loud whistles or magic jackets to conjure up a taxi, and they started to walk.

Suddenly Jake charged ahead. 'There's transport!' He picked up a bike from the pavement. 'It's a City Bike.' He hopped on. 'Let's see if there's any juice left.' He cycled off, dangerously wobbly and then got into his stride. He stopped and yelled back. 'Hop on! We can go to the Brooklyn Bridge – you cannot leave without walking across the Brooklyn Bridge. It would be a crime. C'mon!'

Even in her less than sober state Sandy was unsure. 'Where am I going to sit?'

He banged on the front basket. 'Here. It'll be great.'

She somehow managed to get her backside onto the tray and held her legs out either side. 'Is this a good idea?'

Jake took off, perilously shaky and Sandy held onto the handlebars behind her with a vice-like grip, but they soon got going, staying on the pavement, dodging potholes, not stopping for lights over the deserted streets. The wind flew through her hair and she started to laugh with an abandonment she hadn't felt in years, until they were both shrieking like schoolchildren, flying down Flatbush

Avenue. Jake swung a left, then a right, and they sped on until two tiny dogs, on leashes, flew out from a building and yapped at their heels, their owner running behind them to keep up. Jake braked, the momentum was lost, and they scraped and bumped against a wall which kept them from falling over. Still beside themselves with laughter the dog walker extricated his pets and walked away, shouting 'Crazies!' at them, which made them even more hysterical.

'It's not far now.' They walked unsteadily, occasionally bumping into each other, and climbed the stairs onto the bridge. When Sandy veered off to one side, Jake took her hand and didn't let go, avoiding clashes with infrequent pedestrians who passed them by in the late night. 'That guy was right; it's been a crazy day. Started it drunk three thousand miles away. So much has happened – and I'm drunk again!' Jake drew his hand over his chin. 'I don't feel as exposed as I thought I would, losing the hair. I'm more myself tonight than I've been in years.'

Sandy let go of his hand and spun herself around. 'Me too. I used to be Cassandra Blue but I became Sandy Stuart. Today I'm Cassandra Blue again.' She spun round and round until she noticed Jake had stopped in his tracks. 'What?'

'You're Cassandra Blue?'

'I was. Blue was my maiden name. I became Sandy when I began nursing. Cassandra is a mouthful, apparently.'

'You're Cassandra Blue?' Jake asked again. He ran his hands through his hair and walked around in a circle.

‘Yeah, it’s unusual. Blue is an ancient Scottish name, from Arran. My real name.’

‘You’re the Cassandra Blue who said, “When you look at the stars you are never alone”?’

She stopped dead in her tracks. ‘What? How do you know that?’

‘I saw you on Grampian News. You’d been to see the stars. Your classmates laughed at you.’

‘You don’t need to remind me. It was embarrassing.’ Sandy remembered the day. The local news had joined her class on a school trip to Galloway to observe the night skies. When the observation was complete the journalist had asked them their thoughts on seeing the stars so clearly. Other pupils gave variations of ‘Yeah, it was great,’ or ‘The stars were pure dead brilliant’. Sandy had said she liked it because when you look at the stars you were never alone. Jake was right, her classmates guffawed at her earnestness and continued to guffaw as she’d explained that the vastness of the universe meant humanity couldn't be alone, and there was always someone, somewhere in the world, watching the stars with you.

‘It was both childish and profound. I adored your name. Cassandra Blue. I was still at school and wanted to write a song about you and your words. Never managed it, even though I tried numerous times.’ Jake grappled with his bag and brought out his leather-bound folder. He rifled through the paper and pointed out Cassandra Blue where he’d scrawled it on various sheets. Sandy saw her name, sometimes with her words and then the script would tail off into other lines and drawings. ‘I can’t believe it. I’ve never forgotten it. Always hoping one day I would write… And now – here you are.'

Sandy couldn't believe it either and was trying to get her head around this wild coincidence when she noticed Jake had climbed on top of the railing and was shouting her name to the world.

'Jake be careful. Come down.'

'I've found Cassandra Blue!' he shouted again and nearly lost his footing.

'Please come down.' Sandy was sobering fast.

'Don't you see what this means?' Jake's triumphant expression moved to quizzical – 'Actually, I don't know what it means, but it must mean something!'

'It means you gotta get off the railing.' Neither had noticed two police officers walking towards them.

Jake jumped to the pavement, swaying. 'You don't get it. This is Cassandra Blue. An inspiration!'

'What are you carrying in your hand, sir?'

Jake held it out with a flourish. 'It's a Bic pen. I'm a writer.' He presented an on-guard stance. 'I am Mr Nincompoop and I challenge you to a pen at dawn.' He advanced towards them like a fencing expert. 'C'mon, don't be scared. The pen is mightier than the baton!'

'Whatcha gonna do? Scribble us to death?' The officers cracked up at Jake's foolishness, and one of them used his baton to knock the pen from his hand with an easy tap.

Jake was aghast. 'How did you do that?'

'My friend, that is how we in the NYPD disarm writers.'

Jake bent to retrieve the Bic but lurched forward and was saved from falling over by one of the officers.

'Sorry, Mr Policeman sir. I am drunk in charge of a pen. Arrest me!' and he held his wrists together. The officer took hold of his forearms and pushed them away.

'Ouch. I had a tattoo today.'

Thankfully, both patrol officers were still finding him amusing. 'OK. We have a coupla tourists here who are fried. Where are you from?'

'Scotland.' Sandy replied. 'We flew in this morning, and it's been a long day.'

'Wee, sleekit, cowrin, tim'rous beastie. O, what a panic's in thy breastie!' The officer continued the Burns poem in an atrocious attempt at a Scottish accent.

Jake clamped his hands over his ears. 'Aargh! I charge you with assault of the ears. It's a real crime. Mel Gibson's been charged with it. Christopher Lambert did time for Highlander.'

'Jake, we should stop while we're ahead, or we'll be doing time.'

'Good advice from your inspiration here.'

Sandy took Jake's hand and tried to lead him away.

'Where are you staying?' one of the officers asked.

'The City Hotel. East 34th and Lexington.' She loved saying the address, local style, especially with the leather jacket on.

'OK. Follow us. We'll take you. Save you from yourselves.'

The police officers led them off the bridge to where their vehicle was parked. Sandy and Jake scrambled into the rear seats and with a tiny whoop of the siren, they were off. One of the officers asked them about the sights they'd seen so far and Sandy wittered on about her schedule and how it had gone awry, and they'd delivered a baby, and had tattoos, and been to Bloomies and before the officers could get a word in, they were outside the hotel and Jake's eyes were closed. Thankfully, this time he woke when she nudged him and they crawled out.

'Thanks so much, officers! I take it back about the accent. It was flawless.'

Sandy manoeuvred Jake's head out of the car door and they zig-zagged into the hotel, tumbling into the elevator.

Jake brushed a stray lock of hair behind her ear. 'I can't believe I've found Cassandra Blue.' He bent his head towards her and Sandy couldn't move, terrified he would kiss her, wanting him to kiss her.

He grazed his lips gently against hers, she responded and as his kiss deepened the elevator jolted to a stop and they moved apart. Sandy opened the hotel room door and they flopped onto the bed, immediately crashing out.

CHAPTER 15

Sandy couldn't work out where the banging noise was coming from. She was walking the wards and each time she found the source, it moved somewhere else. At last her addled brain recognised the banging was at the hotel room door and she dragged herself out of her dream. She sat and swung her legs over the side of the bed. A weight in her head clanged forward and hit the front. Ouch. How much had she drunk last night? The knocking on the door continued as Sandy staggered towards it.

'Isobel.'

'Sandy? I've been trying you for ages. I've been so worried.'

Sandy wrestled her phone out of a pocket. Twenty-eight missed calls. She scrolled and saw most of them were from Mike, the others from Isobel.

'Mike called and asked where you were. Can I come in?' Isobel tried to squeeze past but Sandy stayed where she was.

'I've slept through it. Must be the jetlag.'

'Have you been drinking? And where did you get those clothes?'

In the background Sandy heard movement and the bathroom extractor fan went on.

'Who is that?' Isobel covered her mouth with her hand in shock. 'Sandy, what have you been doing?'

'It's nothing. It's a long story. I haven't done anything.'

'Ooooh Sandy!' Isobel giggled, then in a more serious voice said, 'You need to phone Mike.'

Sandy tried to pull herself together. 'How was your day with Chip?'

'He's still here. Do you mind if he joins us today so you can meet him? We're meant to be at the Guggenheim soon; we've missed the rest. As if I needed to remind you!' Isobel wafted her copy of the schedule in Sandy's face.

'No, of course I don't mind. Can I meet you there?'

'OK. I think I'm going to enjoy hearing about your day. You look... So ... un-Sandy.' Isobel was smiling. 'It's good to see you with your hair down, Cassandra.' She hesitated. 'You are alright though?'

'I'm fine, thanks. Hungover.'

'More than two drinks then?'

'I'll see you at 2 pm.'

Isobel walked away, laughing.

Jake was sitting on the bed with his head in his hands. 'It feels worse than it did yesterday, if possible.'

'I desperately need a shower.' Sandy escaped into the bathroom. She ran the shower, brushed her teeth and peeled her clothes off. Her eyes landed on her tattoo. She placed a hand over it protectively. It was precious. How would she explain it to Mike? The phone rang as if on cue.

'Where have you been?' Mike asked. 'I couldn't believe it when Isobel told me you hadn't been together. I was worried about you, being on your own. Why didn't you tell me? Why didn't you answer my calls?' There was a knock on the door. 'Who's that?'

'It's room service; hold on.' Sandy plucked a towel from the rail and squeaked open the door, while holding the phone as far away as possible.

'I'm going to get coffee – want some?'

'No thanks, I'll be fine,' she whispered.

'Won't be long.'

'Mike?'

'Why are you getting room service at this time of day? You should be at the Met – no, the Sistina.'

'I'm sorry, I was tired. I must have passed out. The phone was away in my bag.'

'It's so unlike you. Never mind. You'll be on track now. It's the Guggenheim at 2 pm? Followed by Bloomingdale's.'

'I might not do Bloomingdale's. I might go for a walk or something. Isobel's with Chip.'

'She's got a cheek taking free tickets and leaving you on your own.'

'It's fine, Mike; I said the sightseeing was my treat.'

'You don't sound like you. You didn't answer the room phone either.'

'I was so tired. I didn't sleep on the plane much.'

'I'm sorry I couldn't come. It's been so busy.'

'Mike, I'm going to jump in the shower, I don't have much time to get there.'

'What about the room service? I guess you can take it to go. It'll save time. I'll let you go. Love you.'

'Don't work too hard.' Sandy ended the call and realised she'd forgotten to say 'love you' back.

The hot water in the shower relieved her tense muscles. She couldn't believe how she'd behaved. She'd spent the night on the same bed with a strange man. They'd kissed in the lift. Only a brief kiss, but she remembered the touch of his lips and how deeply she'd felt it. She'd bought clothes. Expensive clothes, not in her style at all. She had a tattoo! Although there was no remorse about the design Etta had created. Explaining it to Mike would be the tricky thing. They never spoke about it, about Carys and the loss they'd both experienced. Sandy dried her hair, trying as best she could to straighten it while her head was so tender. It was soon pinned away. There would be no more nonsense. What was she? A teenager? She applied make-up and stared at her reflection. Cassandra Blue was gone.

How strange that Jake had seen the Grampian interview and remembered her name from more than thirty years ago. He hadn't returned, so she dashed naked to her case and dressed in the suit trousers with a loose-fitting blouse. Her spare schedule was folded in the clothing and she scrabbled for her Sharpie, crossing each item off until the Guggenheim. She had to get herself on track. After the Guggenheim, she would let Isobel and Chip do their own thing together, she was no longer daunted by the idea of being alone. She could meet Isobel later for dinner and the show, Chip could get a ticket and join them. See, she could be flexible. She wrote the plan in her notebook. Removing a bottle of water from the fridge, she drank it with some paracetamol. Desperate for a coffee, she regretted rejecting Jake's offer and was decanting the contents from the pockets of her jacket into her bag when she heard a rustling noise at the door. Opening it, Jake had his hands full of coffee cups and a brown bag in his mouth. She couldn't understand his mumbling and removed it.

'I got us donuts.' She sensed him registering her clothing and hair. 'And I got you a coffee anyway.'

'Thanks, I do need one.'

Placing them on the table, he waved her paracetamol pack. 'May I?'

'Of course.' She took a bottle of water from the fridge and handed it to him. He swallowed some tablets and glugged it all, taking his coffee with him to sit on the bed.

'I've got rehearsals today at Westington Studios. If you fancy coming later, when we finish I could show you the other side of sightseeing.' He smiled at her. 'Off plan, so to speak.'

'I can't. I'm going to the Guggenheim at 2 pm and replacing Bloomingdale's with Bergdorf's, and I've got a Broadway show tonight.'

'Back on schedule then?'

'Yesterday was a mad day. I also need to tell you I've got tickets for the concert tomorrow night. I don't want you to see me in the audience and think I'm some kind of deranged devotee after all. I organised the trip ages ago.'

He frowned. 'Why didn't you say?'

'I don't know, I was angry with you at first and then I forgot.'

'You're coming to the concert on your own?'

'No! My friend Isobel is here too, although she'd met someone online who decided to fly from Houston, so they've been together doing an alternative kind of sightseeing. I'm meeting with her today and we're going to cross a few things off.' She retied the bow at the top of her blouse and buttoned her suit jacket.

Jake watched her. 'Is that how you want to do it? Cross things off?'

She shrugged. 'I'm here to see New York.'

'And didn't yesterday show you the city in a much better way?'

'I want to see the famous sights and it's best with a schedule. It's the only way to fit everything in.'

'I thought—'

Her heart thudded. She couldn't believe she'd been stupid enough not to tell him about Mike. The only way she could think of reacting now was to fight. 'You thought what? A kiss in the lift and spending the day with a rock star might turn my head?'

'No! I thought we had a connection. Yesterday was special for both of us, wasn't it? The kiss – well, we'd had a lot to drink so it didn't really mean anything. Believe me there was no ulterior motive. Didn't you feel it too – that there was something between us? Or have I been a complete numbskull?'

Sandy stayed silent, inexplicably hurt by the fact the kiss didn't mean anything, and also realising how ridiculous this was.

'Numbskull. From 1697 meaning a dull or stupid person.'

'Why do you keep rattling those off?'

'I don't know.' Jake ran a hand through his hair. 'After my life fell apart I called myself so many names for my stupidity, I got into insults, the origins. It's incredibly interesting you know.'

Hands shaking, she ignored him and fussed with her handbag.

'Well, it kept me sane,' he said. 'I'm only saying, meeting you changed me and I think you changed a bit too. This is just one weekend out of the hundreds of weekends in life we'll have; I thought it might be nice to spend it together.'

'I'm sorry. I have plans.'

'So that connection we have – that we've had for years – it doesn't mean anything to you?'

Sandy wished she were someone else, in another time. 'I didn't have the connection. It was only you.'

Jake stared at her for a moment making her squirm inside. 'Then it's been nice meeting you after all these years, Sandy Stuart.'

He walked past her and she heard the click of the door closing behind him.

CHAPTER 16

Sandy was hot, bothered and out of breath when she arrived at the Guggenheim. She was eight minutes past the scheduled time and Isobel tapped an imaginary watch on her wrist when she arrived and smiled. 'Love you being late.'

'Where's Chip?'

'I suggested he go for a walk because I want the details, please.'

'Let's find the café; I need water.' Once they had their drinks, they perched on the edge of a busy table. 'How was it with Chip?' Sandy asked.

'Oh, no, no, no. Spill, lady. What happened? And where did you get the leather jacket. Where's your suit jacket?'

Before leaving the hotel, Sandy had quickly swapped her suit jacket for the leather. 'I bought it yesterday. Don't you think I suit it?'

'I do. It's just ... it's so not your thing anymore. What's going on?'

'Where do I start?' She took a long guzzle of water, not sure how much to tell her friend. Somehow yesterday felt private and personal, and she hadn't had the chance to process Jake's exit and how they'd left things. She didn't tell Isobel who the man was. She made him sound like some random person on the plane who needed help and kept pretty much to the truth about him being drunk and clunking her with a guitar, and the baby, and personal shopping, and the meal. She didn't say anything about the kiss, or Cassandra Blue or how she was a little bit broken inside at the idea they would never meet again.

Isobel hesitated. 'Did you sleep with him?'

'No! We passed out. Honestly. I was – we both were – so drunk.'

Isobel examined her friend's face. 'There's something you're not telling me. Where is he now? Did he want to see you again?'

Sandy played with the zips on her jacket.

'You can't, Sandy. You've been married twenty years. You did tell him you're married?'

'I'm not sure. I mean, he didn't ask.' She grimaced. 'I left it too late. I should have told him from the start.'

'But you and Mike are so good together. Why would you jeopardise that?'

Sandy shook her head. 'We're not good together.' Her eyes filled with tears. 'We're plodding. It's so frustrating.'

It was so obvious that Isobel didn't believe her. 'Where is this coming from? You've never said anything before.'

'I suppose it happens when you've been together a long time. Every day is the same. We've got stuck and I'm so bored with it.'

'Only because you left work too soon. You'll be fine when you go off travelling; it'll be great. You and Mike are made for each other.'

'Are we? Over the years it's like we've consumed each other.'

'Don't say that. All relationships go through bad patches; you don't just let it go because of a bad patch.'

Sandy took another swig of water. 'It doesn't matter. Your turn. How did it go with Chip? And how did he get that name?'

'It's an American thing – Chip off the old block.' Isobel finished her juice. 'He's charming. Kind, considerate and great fun.'

'But...'

'But?'

'I think there's a but coming.'

Isobel took her glasses off and cleaned them. 'He's a totally nice bloke. And we're having a brilliant time.' She wriggled her eyebrows suggestively at Sandy. 'Maybe I'm expecting too much? A special connection is so hard to find.'

Sandy shook her bottle and took a final drink. 'Yes, it is.'

'You and Mike have a lifelong connection. Don't be daft and do something to ruin it, Cassandra.'

Sandy hadn't been thinking of Mike at all. 'I won't. Of course I won't. And why are you calling me Cassandra?'

'There's something reminds me of the you from before. Is it the jacket? You seem more chilled. Your hair is coming loose.'

Sandy tried to get the stray tendrils under control before her friend's watchful eye. Isobel clearly couldn't stop thinking of Mike. 'You cannot give up it all up for a stupid weekend fling in another country!'

'Can't give up what?' said a man behind them. 'Sounds intriguing.'

'Oh! Sandy – this is Chip. Chip meet Sandy.' Sandy saw a tall, handsome, all-American guy and she shook the proffered hand.

'Great to meet you, Sandy. Thanks for being so accommodating while I stole your awesome friend away from you.'

'She had an interesting time on her own, didn't you, my friend?'

Sandy gave Isobel a threatening look. 'It's nice to meet you, Chip. C'mon. Let's go in.'

They made their way round the impressive collection. Sandy's mind was elsewhere, not taking in the artistic display presented to her. She read the information about each artwork but her brain would not retain it. Her head was full of Jake and the day they had spent together.

And the kiss.

Surely it would do no harm. They could be friends, couldn't they? This was an adventure and the kiss meant nothing. Apparently. She would be moving outside her everyday comfort zone – didn't the self-help books always tell her to do that, to confront her fears?

'Sandy!' Isobel was standing beside her. 'I've been calling your name and you've been staring at that description for ages.'

'I'm sorry. I'm hungover. I'm going to go and rest up at the hotel, I'm shattered.'

'You are quite pale. Do you mind if Chip and I go on with the tour? I promise to follow the schedule!'

'You should do the show and dinner, and the cocktails. I'm not up to it – you've got the booking details? I sent a copy of everything.'

'Yes, thanks. But are you sure you want to miss all that? Chip could take off and I'd see him after?'

'I think I need to lie down.' She felt Isobel's beady eye on her.

'Be careful, lovey.'

'I'm tired, nothing more. We'll see each other tomorrow.'

Sandy left them and wandered down Fifth Avenue. She saw her reflection in a shop window and stared. The dress trousers and blouse didn't go with the leather jacket, the ugly walking shoes and handbag even less so. Her hair was dishevelled, with her curls escaping from the clasps. She ducked into Saks, intent on buying a replacement suit – to hell with the cost – and came out in black jeans, a brightly patterned shirt, chic trainers and a backpack. Continuing her meander, she cut across to 42nd Street and entered Grand Central Station. Spotting a bar overlooking the concourse, she ordered water and when it came, asked for a margarita. Something was unravelling and she didn't know how to wind it in again.

The birth of Keisha's baby had touched her deeply. No wonder she and Jake had connected – helping a woman to give birth was exciting and emotional. It wasn't only the baby, though. She was attracted to Jake Cabrelli, the real version, not the boy from the posters and the long-ago dances. The kiss had stirred a deep aching desire untapped for a long time. Why couldn't she bring herself to tell him about Mike? It would have been the obvious thing to do. She wanted to scream, to slither out of her skin and free herself.

Without touching either drink, she paid the bill and left.

CHAPTER 17

Jake thundered along the sidewalk to the studios, his guitar slung over his body, carrying a bag containing replacements of the equipment he'd lost coming over. Halting, he put on his headphones. The cacophony of noise, overwhelming after years of peace and solitude, faded away as he continued walking, enveloped by his own compositions. There was nothing here he could play to the boys though; it was poptastic drivel. He'd lost his music mojo, destined to write pap or produce other people's work. He couldn't even manage one decent song. He tugged his headphones off and allowed the city's constant hum and traffic hoots to assault his ears instead. It was an improvement on listening to his own garbage. He marched to his own beat, steering around fellow pedestrians. *Some people don't know they're alive*, he thought. It wasn't like he'd suggested running away to Outer Mongolia together. Folks were too buttoned up to see the world. Bloody schedules.

And what was this going to be like? The Zoom rehearsals had been better than expected, and they'd recorded all but one of the acoustic tracks for the album.

Why did they need a gig? Whose idea had that been? At least he'd persuaded them a small venue was best; he couldn't have faced a stadium. But he missed the thrill of playing live, the camaraderie with the band, particularly Stu and Danny. It was a pity they hadn't been able to find another singer. Yeah, he and Iain had been civil to each other remotely. It had been ten years. Water under the bridge. What did he care? He cared about Danny, and if it wasn't for him he wouldn't be on his way to rehearsals. And Zaraya would join them on Saturday for a number at the gig, too. Friends again, all forgiven and forgotten.

Not really forgotten.

She'd slept with one of his oldest friends, but years of poring over the ashes of their marriage made him realise how selfish he'd been. Their life had been about his career, ignoring hers, and her career had flown when they split. He'd been a ninnyhammer, an egotistical ninnyhammer. At least his appearance had improved from when he left his cottage and he had decent clothes. But she would notice the extra poundage, that he wasn't the man he used to be. Jake continued stomping, thinking of his rural idyll and how no good ever came from venturing out. He feared it might fall flat tomorrow, and that would be the end of it, for all of them.

He arrived at the studios and tanked through the unprepossessing doorway into reception. Ten years since he'd walked through the doors and he recognised no-one, not bouncers nor the staff behind the desk.

'Jake Cabrelli for The Brig session? It's booked for—'

'Sign here.' The man slid a form across to him. 'Straight through. Expecting many?'

'Four initially, and there'll be more later. Vocal and tech.' Jake signed. 'They'll ask for me or the band.'

'OK. On you go. There're folks in already.'

He moved through the swing doors, his feet treading a once familiar path. The smell of equipment, well-trodden carpets, lost hopes and dreams evoked a tide of overwhelming emotions. He leaned against the wall, shocked at his loss of equilibrium. His belly was full of acid, of hurt and anger from the past. It took a moment to compose himself, then he pushed away from the wall and headed for the main rehearsal room.

'Woah. Mr Giacomo Cabrelli, as I live and breathe, sliding in with two minutes to spare. Not lost your timing?'

'Ha bloody ha.' Jake smiled at the band's bass player, Stu, using the childhood nickname they'd given him.

Danny bashed the drum and crashed the cymbals loudly. 'Great to see you, Jake. Thank the lord you lost the beard. We joked we'd be playing with ZZ Top.' They came over and Jake hugged them, finding comfort in his friends. It was so good to see them, until Danny whispered, 'And thank fuck you've got rid of the kilt. We were going to rip it off you if you hadn't already.'

'Hey! Don't you recognise a fashion statement when you see one?'

Iain came into the room, holding a coffee, and walked over to him. He held out his free hand. 'Jake.'

'Iain.'

They shook hands briefly and there was an uneasy silence. It was Stu who broke it. 'OK, guys. Let's get to it. A lot to get through.'

Danny suggested kicking off with a Bowie track – Jean Genie – like they used to play in the pub circuit days. It would give the audience something unexpected. The others agreed, and Stu suggested they raise the tempo and go for it.

Jake's head was clouded from the night before and he tried to shake off his hangover as he plugged in his guitar and tuned it. Stu did the same. Iain tested his mic and bashed a tambourine against his hip as Danny played a gentle continuous beat in the background.

Finally, they were ready. Jake tapped his foot and counted in. 'One, two, three, four.'

It was loud, it was disjointed and Iain missed vocal cues. 'That's far too fast,' he said to Danny.

'Danny was on the right beat. You were slow. Let's do it again.' Jake tweaked his chords and counted them in as Iain glared at him.

This time it was better, exciting, frenetic - still needed work but there was potential.

'See? Keep up,' Jake said.

Stu interrupted. 'I've created a playlist – shall we give this a try?' He handed out sheets of paper and once settled, the band came in on Jake's cue. They played several numbers and were getting used to being together when Iain interrupted halfway through a song. 'Can we stop a minute? I need a gargle. "Goodbye" has been tricky for me.'

'Thought you'd been working with a coach?' Jake asked.

'I have. Gimme a break.'

Jake shook his head and waited until Iain returned from the bathroom. 'Ready yet?'

'Yup.'

They began again. Iain's voice soared through the ballad, hitting the high notes, sounding terrific.

'Stop. String.' Jake took off his guitar to replace it.

'You should have done it before,' Iain said.

'I didn't know it was gonna break.' He fiddled with the new string.

'I was getting in the groove, man.'

Jake retorted, 'It's hardly on purpose.'

'You sure about that?'

'C'mon guys, time to move on,' Stu said.

'Some of us obviously haven't.'

'I'm here,' Jake said. 'Isn't that enough?'

Iain faced the front. 'Let's go again. Stu, can I borrow your stand? This one's useless.'

Jake was irritated by Iain's pretensions. 'Use your own, you wouldn't even need it if you remembered the lyrics.'

'Take mine. What's going on, Jake?' Stu asked.

Jake threw his hands in the air. 'I've flown three thousand miles; people should have prepared.'

'I am ready,' Iain said. 'My voice has changed over time, like all of us have.'

'What's changed about me?'

'We're ten years older. And my throat was affected during the treatment.'

Jake snorted. 'Rehab, you mean.'

'Yes! Rehab! I'm sorry, I've said I'm sorry.'

'You're sorry – you're *sorry*?' Jake moved over to Iain and knocked the music stand over.

'Great, Jake. Mature. Nice one.' Iain bent to get it but Jake punted it further away.

'Danny!' Stu led the way to the door and they made a quick exit.

Iain walked to retrieve the stand again. Jake petulantly kicked it, hitting him in the legs.

'Fuck's sake Jake, what's wrong with you?'

'What's wrong with me? You're one of my oldest mates and you fucked off with my wife. You were off your face every single day, *off your face*! You were ruining it for us.'

'I'm sorry. I wasn't well, OK?'

'Is that what you called it?'

'It happened, OK. I was a mess; I was a fucking mess. How many times do I have to apologise?'

'Just be professional so we don't have to carry you anymore.'

'You never had to carry me.'

'We had to constantly make allowances for you and we're still doing it.' Iain lunged towards Jake, strategically targeting his jaw. He dodged and as he was a few inches taller, Iain's punch landed weakly on his shoulder. They engaged in a circling dance, ineffectually kicking into space, offering slaps that were more like taps as they darted in and out towards each other.

'You were the one who ran away and put yourself in solitary confinement for ten years,' Iain shouted. 'Wouldn't even talk about it. Asshole coward!'

'You ruined everything with your pathetic drug-addled brain.' Jake threw a blind punch and unfortunately Iain evaded in the same direction, inadvertently moving into the trajectory of the fist, absorbing the full impact on his cheekbone. The force of it knocked Iain off his feet.

Immediately Jake was horrified by his actions. He put his hand out to help Iain, but the singer bounced up off the floor, surprising Jake with his agility, and he found himself pinned against the wall, his breathing hampered by Iain's forearm squeezing into his neck. Jake struggled to push him off as he gasped for air and Iain pushed more weight against him, his teeth bared with effort.

Suddenly Sandy's face appeared over Iain's shoulder, hitting him over the head with his tambourine and clinging to his back with her other arm. She screamed like a banshee,

'Let him go! Let him go!'

Jake was incredulous at the sight before him. Iain released his grip and twirled around trying to get Sandy off, as she hung like a limpet on his back.

'I've let him go,' Iain shouted. 'Get off me!'

Jake prised Sandy off Iain and steered her to one side.

'I'm sorry,' said Iain. His eyes were full of tears and he angrily brushed them away. 'I've been sorry for ten years. I was losing it big time, and I was jealous of you and your bloody songs. My ego got huge and I wanted to go it alone. And yes, I took advantage of Zaraya when she was feeling low. I spent five years in therapy understanding the shit person I'd become. If I could take it back, take it all back, I would.' He took a deep breath. 'I wrote to you a hundred times. I wrote to your Dad. You never once replied.' His eyes were wet again. 'I'm not the same person anymore. I'm not here for the fame or the money. I'm fine. I wanted to be with you, Jake. I wanted my friend in my life again.'

Jake scraped his hands through his hair then covered his face. He walked backwards and crash-sat on an up-ended equipment box, sitting with his head in his hands.

Iain came towards him and laid his hand on his shoulder. 'I am so sorry, Jake.'

Jake sat, feeling the anger that he'd clung to for so long dissipate. 'I'm sorry too.' He flexed his hand and waved it in the air, trying to relieve the sting in his knuckles. 'Sorry for not reading your letters. I was so angry. And hurt. I should've let it go, or not come. Zaraya and I ... we were near the end of the road.' He stood. 'If it makes you feel any better, the song "Cheeky Baby" is mine. That's my limit these days.'

Iain laughed. 'Oh man.' He drew Jake into an embrace. They rocked gently and clapped each other on the back, the way men do.

'C'mon, you guys! Either get a room or give it up,' Stu shouted as he and Danny came through the door.

Jake and Iain stepped away from each other. 'Did you hear that, guys?' Iain asked. 'Jake Cabrelli wrote "Cheeky Baby"' He chuckled.

'Yeah,' Jake said. 'Makes a fortune though.'

‘Can we recommence, gentlemen?’ Stu asked.

‘Wait a minute.’ Jake walked away from the rehearsal area towards Sandy, who had retreated to the back of the hall.

‘Cassandra Blue returns. Part II: The Vengeance!’

‘I figured you needed a damsel to save you in your distress.’

‘Sorry you had to witness that.’

‘I saw Iain leap on you when I came in; I thought he was going to choke you.’

‘It was certainly a well-timed intervention.’ Jake shouted to the stage area, ‘Guys, guys, this is Cassandra Blue.’

Danny bashed out a drum riff. ‘For real? We were sure you were a figment of his imagination.’

Stu came over and shook her hand. ‘Are you really the Cassandra Blue from Dundee?’

‘Yes.’

Iain joined them. ‘You’d make a good bouncer.’

‘C’mon lads. Rehearsals!’ Stu clapped his hands ushering them together. ‘Let’s go.’

‘We’ll be doing a complete run through of the set for tomorrow,’ Jake said. ‘It’s a couple of hours. No encores tonight. Do you want to stay and watch?’

‘I’d love to.’

‘Come and sit here.’ He guided her to a row of seats at the centre of the hall and she watched as Jake steered a path through the masses of leads and various instruments, back to his guitar. Iain took his place behind the mic and sorted through his sheets, placing them on the rack. Stu tuned up. It was strange seeing them together like this, fifteen years or so after the last concert she and Mike had attended. Surreal. She was there as Jake's guest, and just as thrilled as she'd been when she and Isobel had seen them play for the first time at the school dance.

Stu faced the band. 'So are we good now?' There were mumblings from the others. 'I said, are we good? Jake? Iain?'

'Yes! Yes, we are,' they said in unison.

'Good. Let's do it.' He took his place at the other side of Iain. There were a few moments of twanging chords and adjusting buttons and they fell silent. Jake tapped his foot and followed it with, 'One, two, three, four.'

The band went into an energetic version of Bowie's Jean Genie. It was electrifying for Sandy as she listened to Iain passionately belting out the lyrics, backed by Jake and Stu. Her heart pounded in response to the vibrations from the amplifiers and the electric charge permeating the room, the energy potent. She could barely take her eyes off Jake, enthralled by the intensity he exuded as he played and sang.

The Bowie number finished and Stu shouted, 'OK, let's go!'

Jake counted them in and they went into their hit single, "Boys From Nowhere" even more energetically. The single had crawled up the charts and eventually found the number one slot. It stayed there for weeks, the press enthusiastic about the Scottish band from Dundee and their "Beatles-inspired American pop rock with a twist of Scottish country". More familiar singles and tracks followed - she'd forgotten The Brig had had so many hits.

Jake and Stu moved across the stage and played beside each other; next they would move closer to Iain as he sang and sometimes over to Danny as he hit the drums and clashed the cymbals.

Backing singers joined them, and a saxophonist and trumpet. Sandy was fascinated to see how a show comes together, the stopping and starting, the discussions of technical issues, the playing and replaying of choruses. They tried numerous intros as they made decisions about how it would work the next night. She could see how Jake thrived being with the band and how seamlessly they functioned despite an extended time apart.

A modest crowd had gathered to witness the rehearsal, and they applauded at the end of each number, with Sandy joining in. Iain sang "Goodbye", his voice ringing out clear and strong above the instruments and when it ended, the band joined in the applause. During the set, Sandy was impressed to see Jake move easily from guitar to violin, mandolin and even a turn on keyboards. More numbers, including "Lonely Days" and "Pretty Girl Summer", two of Sandy's favourites, brought them to their last chart hit "Dance with Time", a rocky number with a funky brass undertone, up-tempo and rousing. The band belted it out – at one with each other, in their element, loving the music they made. Sandy watched Jake singing in the chorus and he smiled at her, making her heart flip. Later he played his guitar solo; with his eyes closed, his fingers ran over the strings and the chords he played pulsed through her soul, sending shivers through her body. The session complete, the audience whooped and clapped, and the band applauded too. Sandy watched as Jake and the others put their instruments away and moved through the visitors, shaking hands and chatting with old friends and colleagues.

Jake waved at Sandy and held up his hand to say five minutes, as The Brig huddled together, talking quietly.

'OK,' Jake said and broke away calling out, 'tomorrow we have a full set run through again at the venue with tech, vocals and the brass – plus sound check. From 2 pm.' He waved to a mezzanine section holding the sound engineers. 'Thanks, guys.'

A young woman dressed trendily in black called out: 'Sorry Jake, make that 1 pm please. There're some interviews from MTV to go with the EPK and TV broadcast so I need you there prompt. Gear will be transported from here to the venue, so it'll be waiting for you. It will also be taken to the recording studios for Sunday's session – and if you've given me a list, where you want it to be sent on from there. Thanks all. See you tomorrow.'

Jake came over to Sandy. 'How did we sound?'

Sandy had watched the Jake she'd met yesterday metamorphosise into his rock and roll persona. She'd become a middle-aged fangirl, crushing on the man and guitar, so aware of his presence. 'It was exciting to see you play. And so close. It was energising, inspiring...' She trailed off, tongue-tied and awkward, and was saved by Iain.

'Here you are, the real-life Cassandra Blue. Nice to actually meet you.' He held his hand out to Jake. 'It was something else, wasn't it, playing together again? It's gonna be spectacular tomorrow.'

Jake shook Iain's hand. 'Yeah. Tomorrow will be even better.' He turned to Sandy. 'Shall we go and do some sightseeing?' They moved towards the exit, where Jake stopped next to Stu and Danny.

'Are you gonna stay in New York for a while?' Danny asked.

Jake shook his head. 'I've got a flight back on Monday morning. I can do anything from my studio.'

'Ach, it's not the same on your own. Come back to NY, man. We could jam and work on another album.'

'Yeah, we've missed you buddy. It would be great to hangout. Get a few beers occasionally,' Stu remarked.

'Doesn't beat the wilderness,' Jake said.

'The man wants his lair. At least you're no longer the wild man of Angus,' Danny said. 'Your influence, Cassandra?'

'All his own doing.'

Danny and Stu took turns hugging Jake.

'Great to see you in the flesh, Giacomo,' Danny said.

CHAPTER 18

As Sandy came through the exit behind Jake, photographers rushed forward, surrounding them and clicking away with their cameras.

'How was it with Iain and the guys, Jake?'

He put a protective arm around Sandy and steered her away. The photographers ran round in front of them, and she could hear and see the flashes going off as she hurried to keep pace with him.

'I heard there was a fight. Zaraya there, too?' One of the photographers followed for a while, trying to get a shot of Jake. He covered his face to thwart any image and as they rushed across the road, the paparazzi were left behind.

'That was scary.'

'That's nothing. Should've seen it in our heyday. We loved the attention at the beginning, then hated it.'

As they walked further away, she sensed a degree of tension leaving Jake. He ran his hands through his hair and zipped his jacket. 'So,' he said. 'You ready to see how the other half sightsee?'

'You've got big competition – tonight was cocktails and dinner at the Buzz Bar and after, a Broadway show.'

'You've already had the show. In fact you had two for the price of one. I'm not scared of being mugged with you around, you'd make a brilliant bodyguard!'

'I don't know what came over me.'

'Neither did Iain. I bet his head is still ringing.' Jake sniggered. 'The least I can do is buy you dinner. We could head towards Chelsea for food, take a mooch around the area. There're some indie art galleries open there late into the night and it's a great vibe.'

'You're the guide.'

'Have you been on the subway yet?'

'No. I've been very extravagant with taxis today.'

'We'll go to Canal Street.' Jake made a left. 'This is Chinatown we're in now.' There was no mistaking it; neon building signs in Chinese script flashed into the dusk and brightly coloured lanterns were strung across the road, casting an eerie light on the pedestrians.

Jake led them to the subway and tapped them both through the turnstiles onto the platform. They stepped inside the busy train and were hurtled along the track. Sandy could see Jake behind another passenger, scrolling through his mobile. *Positively pulchritudinous*, she thought and reddened when he looked up and caught her eye. They exited onto 13th Street and passed Jackson Square where an operatic busker had drawn a small crowd.

'This is the Meatpacking district around here – great for late clubs and live music bars. And very posh apartments and shops. We're going on to Chelsea Market.'

Inside they wandered the eateries and chose dishes from the wide variety on offer. Sandy's mouth exploded with heat from the jerk chicken and she needed a few glugs of beer to cool things down. Jake was impervious to the hot chillies in the dishes. She fared better with the Chinese food, but he had to give her a lesson with chopsticks. They spoke of their favourite foods, what they liked to create.

'I only learned to cook the last ten years,' Jake said. 'Food delivery options are limited where I am and it's cold by the time it arrives. I'm a dab hand in the kitchen these days – my signature dish is Bulgogi.

'What's that?'

'Korean dish that translates to "fire meat". We played Soeul a few times and I loved it. The secret is in the marinade and the kimchi. I've even got my own special griddle now.

'Sounds delicious.'

'I should have taken you to a Korean place. Next time.' Sandy felt the hairs rise on the back of her neck as a thrill worked its way through her at the idea there might be a next time.

They lingered in the small galleries that were still open. Sandy could see a whole world of creativity, one she hadn't found in the Guggenheim or any other huge art museum she'd visited in the past. The area was bursting with art and life in a way she hadn't experienced before and she felt provincial and uneducated. But turning a corner, Sandy was delighted to see the work of a collage artist she admired, Maya Bharoo. The window had a large display of the artist's collages, created from hundreds of faces, cut and stuck together. She peered in closely, intrigued by the smaller faces fashioning the whole, disappointed the gallery was closed.

'I love her work,' she said. 'For me it shows all the individual people we can be, however the mosaic is put together. God, listen to me, I sound like that naïve schoolgirl on Grampian TV again.'

'No, you don't. It's fascinating work, the amount of faces and scenes you can see.'

'It was used as a demonstration in a psychotherapy lecture I went to. She created art to counter mental health difficulties she was dealing with.'

Sandy regarded their own faces reflected in the window, close together, almost touching. Their eyes met and Jake gently pushed a tendril of hair behind one ear.

'Shall we find somewhere for a nightcap?' he asked. 'There're plenty of bars to choose from.' They walked on and found a restaurant with tables outside, the air mild and quite humid as they took seats and a waiter emerged.

'Another beer? Hold on - here's something you should try.' Jake asked the waiter. 'Do you do Apple Martinis?'

'Yes sir, we do. Two?'

'Yes, thanks.' The waiter went off. 'Then I'll take you home.'

The idea of heading to the hotel saddened Sandy, she didn't want the night to end. 'Was it cathartic, having it out with Iain?'

'Maybe. Mostly embarrassing that I lost it – again. We haven't been in a room together since the fight on stage. Jeez, we carry a lot of angry shit, don't we?'

The waiter came with their drinks.

'Try it,' Jake said.

Sandy took a sip. It was ice cold and refreshing, a fresh fruity flavour and there was a kick behind it too. 'Mmm. Delicious.'

'Here's to you. I couldn't believe it when your face appeared, it was so out of place.' He mimicked a double take. 'Whacking him with his own tambourine. The vision will amuse me for a long time.' Jake clinked his glass against hers. 'It must be this weekend's rock chick vibe.'

'Must admit I'm a split personality here. I don't know quite who I am anymore.' She sipped her drink. 'So, "Cheeky Baby", eh?' She needed to move the subject away from herself.

'I wondered how long it would take you to mention that song!' Jake said. 'Not my best. So successful though, more than the other hits combined. I wrote it one night when I'd had far too much whisky, sitting alone, being maudlin. I did the whole thing in about an hour, the worst lyrics ever! The next day I asked old friends of mine to come and sing it. I wanted them to be like the Cheeky Girls so we called them The Kittens after kitten heels. It was great fun. I used a pseudonym; no-one guessed it was me. There've been more for other acts. They charted, too. Nothing decent though – nothing for the guys. Stuck in middle-of-the-road cheese.'

'I think you're being hard on yourself. What happened today with Iain could be helpful. Sometimes confrontation is needed to move forward. Conflict resolution works; I've read a lot about it this past year.'

'Are you trying to psychoanalyse me?' Jake waggled his fingers at her like a faux hypnotist.

Sandy laughed. 'I'm interested in the subject, that's all. I've been considering studying as a counsellor or psychotherapist, to work with mothers. Supporting women when they're pregnant and giving birth when they're at their most vulnerable. For some it's straightforward and happy, like Keisha; for others it's more difficult – perhaps because of poverty or other issues. It's not always about class or social problems. Pregnancy and birth are a leveller; it doesn't matter where you're from, anything can happen.'

Jake tapped her glass with his. 'You'd be good as a counsellor. I watched you yesterday, so calm and caring, lost in the rhythm of the baby's birth. The whole thing blew my mind.'

'Same with your music today, you playing – the energy – vital and vibrant and full of life.'

Jake put his glass next to Sandy's and their hands touched and stayed touching. 'The beauty of any form of creativity. Even an Apple Martini.'

'Being here makes anything possible, for some reason. I've never been to the US before; it's the size of it that's so appealing.' Sandy finished her drink.

'It's called the land of opportunity for a reason. Shall we go?'

Jake got his wallet out but Sandy pushed it away. 'This is on me. You don't need to pay for everything.' With the bill settled, they headed off into the night, the city still awake, shops and bars with open doors spilling light onto the sidewalks. They arrived at a subway station and, with one change, were rattled in busy carriages across town to 34th Street. They came out to a rainstorm with water streaming over the steps of the exit. Jake removed his jacket and held it over their heads as they ran for the hotel, but the rain was too heavy and they took cover under an awning. Sandy watched the rain hammering the tarmac and flooding into the drains, the lights of the passing cars reflected in the rain-slicked pavements.

'Still can't believe *the* Jake Cabrelli wrote that song.' Sandy quoted lines, '*Don't tell me you want me, 'cos I'll tease you; Don't tell me you need me, 'cos I'll leave you.* People were singing it at the airport when we left.' she laughed. *'Cos I'm a cheeky baby!'*

'You see! It may be fromage but once it's in your head you can't get it out. It was a worldwide hit – if only we'd had as much success as the band, although we did well enough.'

'You were huge!'

'And the next bit?' he asked quietly. "Can you remember the next line?"

Sandy found it difficult to speak, only managing to whisper, 'I think it's: *If you kiss me baby, kiss me good. Kiss me like I know you could...*' She couldn't move as he looped a curl of her hair round his finger. He was so close she could feel his warm breath on her cheek.

'I love your hair; you shouldn't tuck it away.' He kissed Sandy and the touch of his lips trembled through her as she kissed him back. He kissed her neck, her face, her eyes then found her lips again. Desire surged inside her, waves of longing rocked her body.

'Do you want to...?' He kissed her again and when he broke free she whispered, 'Yes.' They moved out into the rain and Jake slipped a hand round her back; it burned against her skin under the shirt. At the entrance he drew her to him. 'Are you sure?' Sandy stared into his eyes. This would be the time to tell him about Mike. His name was on the tip of her tongue, yearning to be let out. But she couldn't do it. She wanted so much to be with this man tonight.

'It's just one weekend out of all the weekends, isn't it?' she said.

Taking her hand, Jake led the way into the hotel.

CHAPTER 19

Sandy lay awake in the darkness listening to the steady breathing of the man beside her. Her body tingled from his touch. It had been delicious to be so wanted, and to want someone so badly, so physically, it hurt. They had undressed each other in the dark, their bodies softly illuminated by the light from the street, and explored each other with hands and mouths. She trembled, remembering how her body had ached for him, her inhibitions lost in fiery desire. His gentle strokes had easily aroused her, and she'd responded ardently, loving his big body, its strength.

Mike drifted into her head, the perfunctory couplings they'd been reduced to as the eagerness of their early years was lost in the goal of having a child. She pushed the guilt away.

Jake shifted in his sleep, turning towards her and she was free to examine his face. Awake, there was an undercurrent of tension in his features but there was no sign of it now. Sandy lay in the dark. This was madness, with no future. She would return to Mike, and Jake to his rural cottage, but like his friends, thought it would be a shame if he continued to hide himself away. When she got home, she would hold this experience to her, take strength from it and find a way forward with Mike. In this moment, she would relish every second.

'Can't sleep?' Jake inched closer and nuzzled into her neck. 'I still can't believe it's you. I saw you all these years ago and the memory of you stayed with me.'

'I saw you too, though. You played at our school before you were famous. Isobel and I were devoted fans. She was in love with Iain and when we could pass for eighteen, we'd come to the pub gigs.'

'And who did you fancy – was it Iain too? Or was it Stu? When we made it, the girls loved Stu. Or was it me?' He fluttered his eyelashes at her and preened.

Sandy couldn't stop herself blushing as she remembered the Cabrelli-club fanatic she'd been. 'It was you. I had a crush on you.'

'Did you now!' He held her closer. 'Did you have a poster on your wall? Did you have a jotter with my face on it?'

Sandy squirmed.

'You did! I can't believe it. A real fan.'

'Stop it!

He smiled and kissed her again.

When she woke in the morning it was to find Jake beside her writing in a notebook. She went to the bathroom and tried to alleviate her guilt by texting Mike good luck for his London meeting, realising too late that with the time difference, it was long over. She'd heard nothing from him. Isobel was happy to be spending time with

Chip and wasn't asking too many questions, only admonishing her to be careful. Chip had managed to get a ticket for the concert from an agent, spending hundreds of dollars more than the original value Sandy had paid when the gig was announced. Jake would be busy pre-concert, so she'd arranged to meet them at the restaurant as planned.

Sandy stepped in the shower. Who was this lunatic that had taken over her body for the weekend? She'd never once thought of being unfaithful in all their years together. What was she doing? But when Jake joined her in the shower, it was so natural being with him, she was powerless to resist. He soaped her body until she was quivering for him, unused to being so sexually alive. He lifted her easily, and her guilt was banished by passion.

Later, they got dressed and Jake, ready to leave, drew her into a hug and whispered in her ear. 'Last night was beautiful.' He kissed her again. 'I'll see you after the concert. Meet me at the side entrance, you'll find it easily.' Sandy agreed and he left.

CHAPTER 20

She dressed in her rock-chick outfit of jeans, leather jacket and boots. The cost had been hideous, although the pleasure was worth it. Outside, the day was clear and fresh, with no sign of the thunderclouds from the night before. She was wearing the top Camille had chosen for her and wanted something fresh, so bought another funky bright shirt from a boutique on Fifth Avenue on her way to Central Park. She wore it immediately, loving its glorious colours – so refreshing from the beige and creams that had become her staples. She smiled at the dent that this weekend was making in her bank balance, finding she didn't care. All the years she'd saved, hoping for a child to spoil, had given her a financial freedom she hadn't contemplated before.

'You look completely different. Is it the clothes?' Isobel examined her as she sat at the table they had booked months ago.

'It's the jeans and bright colours. I'm giving up the neutrals. Where's Chip today?'

'He'll be here in a minute. He's great, like a big lolloping teddy bear, but I didn't realise it would be so full on. I hope you don't mind but you seemed quite happy to be on your own?'

'It's been... liberating in a way.'

'You're glowing. And it's not only the clothes, is it?'

Sandy smiled. 'I feel independent. Self-sufficient. Being here makes me feel alive.'

'You slept with him, didn't you?'

Sandy opened her mouth to lie but she couldn't.

Isobel's face was pale. 'Sandy, how could you? Who is this guy?'

'I've had a bit of fun, something I haven't had for a long time.'

'You have fun with Mike!'

'Not really. It's not the same.'

Isobel's eyes filled with tears. 'I don't want to see you throwing your marriage away.'

'I won't.'

'This is insane. Will you see this guy when you get home?'

'No! It's just this one weekend, then I'll go home to Mike.'

There was a long pause, neither friend wanting to look at the other, then Isobel said, 'I always imagine you and Mike are how Brian and I would be if he had lived.'

'I'm sorry Isobel, but we can't be what you want us to be. Mike and I ... it's like we're floundering.'

Sandy was relieved when Chip joined them at the table and ended the conversation. Initially annoyed that she wouldn't have this night alone with her friend, he was now saving her from probing questions. Isobel was right, he was like a big teddy bear, with his floppy blond hair, big smiles and wholesomeness. He entertained Sandy with their sightseeing stories: the buggy ride round Central Park, the walking tour of St Patrick's, the Broadway show the night before. His enthusiasm and enjoyment for everything they'd seen lifted the mood at the table.

'Tonight is on me. We've been using all the tickets you'd bought for today's sightseeing and I need to thank you.' he said.

It was a busy Italian diner that Sandy had booked, having found it in a gourmet guide to NYC. She ordered Apple Martinis for them all. The pasta was delicious, the atmosphere busy and cheerful. Chip ordered another round of martinis and after savouring their drinks and feeling a pleasant high, they made their way to the venue.

The line was long already and they joined it, basking in the evening sunshine. Chip went off to find beers while they waited. Sandy watched the crowd, much the same generation as themselves, some sporting band T-shirts from past tours. A woman walked by wearing a pair of vintage sunglasses with Jake's face reflecting in the lenses. A pang of jealousy rang through her. Was she just another fan?

'I have a little surprise for you.' Isobel thumbed through her phone, finding a photo she wanted and held it out to Sandy. 'Remember this?' There they were, seventeen years old and taking photos in a booth on the way to a Brig concert. Isobel's hair was short and spiky, next to Sandy's blonde, unruly curls. The amateur poses they'd struck trying to appear trendy, showed them as twee and uncool – but fun to see. And the make-up! How much blusher and eyeliner had they ladled on? There were four shots in total, variations of the same silly poses. 'Look at us!' Isobel zoomed into the grainy pictures.

They hooted at the clothes and how unbelievably young they were, any tension from their earlier conversation forgotten in the joy of their longtime friendship and shared fandom. Isobel swiped on to the next one – she was posing in front of a poster of Iain with her tongue out, licking his mouth.

'I remember that night! It's when we bought the band paraphernalia, pens and notebooks and stuff. God we were diehards,' Sandy said.

Isobel flicked on and there was Sandy, beside a poster of Jake, with her hands together formed in a heart in front of her.

'Aw, sweet – you were so mad about him.' Isobel smiled, but Sandy was close to tears seeing her younger self and remembering the infatuation she'd had. Is that what she was doing? Enacting an immature crush? She shivered, a sadness coming over her and she no longer wanted to bring out the pictures she'd taken, worried she might give something away. She gave Isobel a hug. 'I'm so glad we're together tonight.'

The queue inched forward and Chip brought over their beers. They drank them surreptitiously, like the naughty schoolgirls they once were. Isobel's excitement was contagious and Sandy couldn't help but absorb the elevated energy in the crowd, lifting her mood.

At the entrance, they stuffed their empty bottles in a bin, and soon they had passed security and into the hall. They found a spot close to the front, but far enough away from the stage to see them properly. The intimate venue filled quickly and the noise of the crowd talking rose to a feverish pitch as they waited with anticipation.

The stage was in darkness, and figures dressed in black could vaguely be seen moving around, checking instruments and equipment. The crowd stilled in expectation. A spotlight came on in the centre of the stage and earned its own cheer from the audience then the stage was dark again. Sandy's heart was beating fast and she pined at being so far from Jake when they'd been so close the night before.

Another bright spotlight appeared at the side of the stage and this time the audience was quiet. A man holding a microphone stepped into the light; Sandy recognised him from the rehearsal audience.

'Good evening, New York! How are y'all? Ready for a good night?' The audience roared. 'It's my greatest pleasure to introduce – for one exclusive night only – the Scottish band you've been waiting to hear from for ten long years. Please give us your loudest for Iain, Jake, Danny and Stu – *The Brig!*'

The crowd went wild, whooping and whistling. The man's key light went dark and other spots came on with the band in position. The audience roared as Jake and Stu made final checks to their guitars.

Iain spoke. 'We are so psyched to be here, where we played our first ever US gig. Can you believe it was twenty years ago? Thank you for coming to our reunion.' His words were met with an even more boisterous response. 'We're kicking off with a tribute to a man who is close to our hearts and – close to you New Yorkers – David Bowie.'

Jake counted them in and they exploded into the number. It was even more dynamic than the rehearsal. Iain belted out the fast lyrics. The crowd cheered enthusiastically, drawn into the band's cover of "Jean Genie". It was a rip-roaring way to launch the show. Towards the last verse, the tempo slowed and the anticipation in the crowd hummed as the song gathered pace again, exuding an energy that crackled round the auditorium. Iain screamed and bawled the last lines out and Danny and the guitars rocked loudly on the outro.

'Thank you, Bowie,' said Iain.

Iain and Jake counted the next number in together – "The Boys From Nowhere" – and Sandy sang every word. She could see Jake scanning the crowd until his eyes rested on her, and he smiled.

Isobel jumped. 'Oh my God Sandy – Jake Cabrelli looked at you, he smiled at you!' she yelled in her ear. Sandy grinned at Isobel who pogoed like a punk teen, and Chip joined in.

The Brig played on, the enthusiastic crowd giving the loudest appreciation they could, applauding and whistling. Sandy was transfixed – Jake's energy, the movement of his body, his hands on his instruments – the way those hands had played her body the night before. She ached with longing. Iain introduced the next track and they played as roving lights danced over the stage and spotlit the singer, Zaraya, who was waiting in the wings. She was luminous with her twinkling Afro hair, gravity defying earrings and shimmering mini dress. The woman had star power in spades and she walked on to the stage to loud cheers, including Sandy's, and took her place beside Iain. Her sensational voice rang out in harmonic contrast to the lead singer's.

Sandy watched Jake singing happily with his ex-wife on stage. It was an extended version of "Lonely Days", a rich rocky number blending the guitars and brass with backing vocals, and a key change built on the emotional resonance of the words. Zaraya sang with Iain, moved to Stu's mic for a while, and over to Jake's. Sandy watched as they sang the chorus together, aware of how hurt Jake had been by their breakup. Zaraya shimmied to the front of the stage beside Iain, her voice soaring exquisitely, dancing from side to side, talent radiating from every pore. The number finished and the band applauded with the crowd, as Zaraya took her bow and left the stage.

Sandy was aware the band had reached the closing numbers and watched Stu and Danny leave the stage, wondering if there'd been a technical hitch. Iain spoke to the crowd from the side.

'This one's a solo number from Jake. It's called "Cassandra Blue"'.

Sandy's heart leapt into her mouth.

Isobel grasped her in disbelief. 'OMG. The guy you've been seeing. Is it Jake Cabrelli?'

Sandy couldn't hear, could only read her lips and nod. Isobel's eyes bulged but Sandy was only aware of Jake.

With his acoustic guitar as accompaniment, he sang a soft gentle ballad, telling of love over time, as constant as the stars, and the chorus spoke of never being alone when you can share the stars and skies with those you love. Jake was gazing at her as he sang and she was transfixed. The power of his words moved her; he'd written this for her. About her. Her eyes filled as she listened to the lyrics and heard the love Jake had in his voice.

Time stopped as she gazed out at him from the audience and his voice caressed her heart. Jake moved into a second chorus and Sandy was jolted out of the spell he had cast when a pair of arms wrapped around her from behind. She twisted around and there was Mike.

'You didn't think I'd miss this, did you?' he said, hugging her to him and he kissed her lips.

Sandy felt as though she was going to faint. He faced her to the front again so she could watch the stage, his hands around her waist, his chin resting on her shoulder. She couldn't move, feet cemented to the spot, sick with disappointment, her heart pounding so heavily in her chest she feared people would hear it.

Jake, whose eyes had been closed as he sang the chorus looked at her again and faltered slightly. He continued with a raw emotion to his voice, lost in his own melody, concentrating on his guitar. The track finished and the enthusiastic crowd whooped and whistled their appreciation. With the rest of the band taking their places they blasted into "Pretty Girl Summer" and this time Sandy barely registered it as one of her favourites. Her mouth was dry and her eyes were filled with tears.

Mike hugged her to him and shouted in her ear, 'I was in London and saw a New York flight was leaving at the same time. I went mad.' He was extremely pleased with himself and Sandy's legs were so weak she had to lean against him. She was having an out-of-body experience as the gig went on around her and she disengaged from the scene. How could she convey anything to Jake from that distance? She stood, motionless, still in shock.

Iain introduced their last song of the night, another hit from their successful catalogue and the crowd joined in. He stopped singing and held the mic out to the audience where they regaled him with a verbatim, albeit slightly out of tune, version of the chorus. Applause for an encore brought the band to the stage twice more. Jake didn't look again in her direction, concentrating on his playing and singing. How could she tell him about Mike now? Or why he was here. To be able to say something about how much the words and music he'd written meant to her.

As the band took their last bows Jake left the stage, his face inscrutable.

CHAPTER 21

As they moved with the crowd towards the exit, Sandy managing to pull one trembling foot in front of the other and act naturally towards Mike, who was so proud of his impromptu appearance. All she could think about was why he'd picked that one moment in their lives to do something impetuous. And, more importantly, had he heard the introduction to Jake's solo?

Once outside, Isobel quickly did the introductions. 'Chip this is Mike, Sandy's husband,' underlining his status with a meaningful look, standing in front of Mike so he couldn't see. Sandy had no idea if Isobel had told Chip anything but was happy to see her friend was on alert.

Mike indicated a lively bar across from them but, worried the band might choose somewhere local after the concert, Sandy suggested going to the hotel lounge. Once there they could relax about getting home, she persuaded them. She led the way to the subway, tapping Mike through as Jake had done for her. The train was busy and noisy – Saturday night in New York – and conversation was limited as they tried to speak over the general hubbub and rattle of the train. Once at the City Hotel, they headed to the bar.

Sandy dragged Isobel to the loo with her. 'Does Chip know?

'No specifics, although I might have let something slip about you being naughty...'

'You didn't?' Sandy stared at her friend in the mirror.

'I'm sorry, I mean who would believe Mike would turn up!' Isobel asked.

Sandy covered her face with her hands. 'Oh God, I can't even remember the things I've told him.'

'And I can't believe your guy is Jake Cabrelli. Why didn't you tell me it was him?'

'It's been so unreal, like a dream.' Sandy could sense Isobel's hurt. 'I'm sorry. I don't know what I'm doing. I've been all over the place this weekend.' Sandy closed her eyes and took a long shaky breath.

'Listen, Chip and I will have one swift drink and go,' said Isobel. 'That way he's less likely to say anything untoward, although I'm sure he wouldn't. Then that leaves you with Mike.'

Sandy liked having a plan and they arrived at the bar where Chip and Mike already had the drinks and were discussing the gig.

'I'd heard of them but never really listened to their music,' said Chip. 'They might play in Texas – you could come over, Isobel. I could show you around there.'

Isobel yawned. 'Sorry.' She covered her mouth. 'I'm so tired. Why don't we take our drinks to our room, Chip?'

Obviously disappointed at ending the night early, Chip cheered up when Isobel took his hand and kissed his cheek. 'Great meeting you, Mike,' he said.

Isobel squeezed Sandy's shoulder and they said their goodnights, leaving Mike and Sandy alone. She took out her phone. 'How long can you stay? I can amend my return flight to yours.'

'I'm leaving tomorrow afternoon, flying to London for a meeting on Monday.'

'What? You came over for one night?'

He hugged her. 'It was a moment of madness.'

'Surely you could ask them for two or three days' leave? It makes no sense.'

'Don't be angry, Sandy. I wanted to see you; it's our anniversary and when I saw the timings of the flights I bought a ticket on impulse. It cost a fortune, though.' Mike laughed. 'Thank goodness you organised my visa at the same time as yours!'

Sandy had forgotten all about their anniversary, and the visa. 'I managed to get a ticket from a tout outside the gig. His luck was in, the concert was almost over. That cost a fortune too!' He tittered to himself, beyond pleased with his spontaneity. 'The Brig were brilliant - even if I did only catch two-and-a-half tracks and the encores.' He took a sip of his beer. 'Jake Cabrelli doesn't usually do solos, does he?'

Sandy mumbled into her drink.

'You're so different tonight, Sandy. Your hair. The clothes. You have a glow about you, sweetheart. It reminds me of when we first met.'

She ignored that. 'To be honest, with Isobel being with Chip, I've had a quiet time, walking around everywhere, kind of doing my own thing.'

'A schedule's the best way to sightsee, remember.'

'I suppose I wanted to try things another way, left to my own devices. Do you want to go to the room? You must be shattered.' As she spoke her mind raced, trying to remember whether there was anything of Jake's there.

'I'm not even sure where I am at the moment, it's bizarre the time lag and rushing from the plane to be at the concert.' Mike drank his beer. 'I can't even remember where we are in the city!'

Inside her hotel room Sandy was relieved to see the bed had been remade with fresh sheets and there was nothing to indicate the time she and Jake had spent there. She removed her jacket and boots and stretched out her long legs. 'Are you sure you can't stay any longer?'

'No. I have to go to this meeting; the financiers will be there and I have to give them a report and confirm it'll be finished in time.'

'You can't Zoom?'

'No. It's better if I'm there, they need the detail and they might have questions. I only wanted to surprise you.'

'You certainly did.' Guilty at her lack of appreciation of Mike's grand gesture, she went over and kissed his cheek. He hugged her. 'It is good to see you, Mike.'

'You too. Even though I almost don't recognise my wife.' He ran his hands gently over her arms, then stopped.

'What's this?'

'I got a tattoo, it's the dressing.'

'A tattoo! You've never said anything about wanting a tattoo.'

She took her arm out of the sleeve and peeled off the clingfilm, and there in its small perfection was Etta's delicate work.

'Carys.' Mike drew his finger softly across the design. 'Did it hurt?'

Her eyes filled with tears and it was a moment before she could answer. 'Not as much as us never talking about it.'

He turned away and she knew he was finding it as difficult as she was. 'I didn't think you wanted to.'

'I tried. You always brushed me off. We drifted our separate ways. Keeping it inside. It hurt so much, Mike.'

'I know how much it hurt. I lost Carys too.' He took her hand and kissed it; tears in his eyes. 'I felt so useless, not being able to give you the child you wanted.'

'You wanted children too.'

'I was the one with the low sperm count.' He let go of her hand and wiped his face. 'It made me feel so utterly inadequate whenever we made love.'

'Mike!' When she reached out to him again he moved away. 'I took Viagra because I was so worried about not being able to perform when I needed to.' He sank on the bed.

'Oh, Mike.'

'It was my fault. I could see how awful it was, the treatment you went through time and again and you never complained. Never said you blamed me.'

'Because I didn't. It never entered my head to blame you. I blamed myself for not being able to give you a baby. The miscarriages. I couldn't be a proper wife to you.'

'You were always my wonderful wife. Always. And when you were pregnant with Carys, I was so frightened for you, for us, scared to hope. In the end when we lost her my heart broke, for you and for Carys. I wanted to be strong for you. You were the one who'd carried her inside you.'

Sandy drew him to her, rocking him gently as years of her husband's hidden suffering was released.

They lay for an hour, holding each other. There was no need to speak; everything was understood. Eventually Sandy climbed off the bed. 'Why don't you have a shower and I'll make you some tea before you sleep?' she asked. 'It's ridiculous o'clock for you.'

'Good idea. I'll get something from room service, I'm hungry now.' He regarded the menu. 'They only serve between 5 pm and midnight. Didn't you get room service yesterday?'

Her stomach tightened with panic, remembering his call the day before, when Jake was there with her. Before she could answer he scratched his head and said, 'Or was it today?' He shrugged. 'I'm so confused. I'll be better after a shower.'

Mike went off to the bathroom and Sandy got into her white cotton nightdress, grateful for the reprieve. He finished showering as she brushed her teeth, her hair pinned out of the way. She remembered being with Jake less than twenty-four hours ago and shook her head to banish the memory.

In the bedroom they sat on the easy chairs, sipping tea.

'When is your flight tomorrow?' she asked.

'Six pm. We could do the schedule and I could go to the airport after we've had lunch. I checked, a taxi should only take—'

'Forty-two minutes.' They said it in unison and smiled at each other.

'I'm going to turn in, try and get a few hours' kip,' said Mike. 'I watched three-and-a-bit films on the flight. Didn't sleep. Coming?'

'I'll finish my tea. I'm awake now, must be the jet lag for me, too. It does strange things to you.'

Mike climbed into bed and instantly dropped off. Sandy stared out the window, aware Jake was somewhere in the teeming city. So close yet so far away. She wished she had his phone number, though she knew how bad she'd feel, messaging him while her husband slept.

She remembered the song he'd written for her, inspired by her long-ago trip to see the dark skies. It had touched her in a way she'd never experienced. It was as well Mike had appeared because she was dangerously close to losing her heart. Was Jake with Zaraya tonight? There was a star more real than anything she'd seen in the sky that Galloway night.

Whatever he felt about Zaraya, it only underlined how Jake's world was not her world. His talent would take him to places she could never be part of, not if she were honest with herself. At the end of the day, she was Sandy

Stuart. No longer Cassandra Blue. She wished she could see him though, explain about Mike – she didn't want him to think... What? What didn't she want him to think? That she'd lied to him? She had, by omission. Why had she denied her husband? Because Jake had been such an asshole in the beginning and his barbed comments hit the mark; because being alone this weekend had changed her, because she'd discovered a side of herself she hadn't seen for a long time.

Sandy got into bed beside her husband, clicked off the light and lay listening to his breathing, guiltily remembering Jake and the rhythms he had played on her body. Her eyes closed and as dawn rose over the skyline, she fell into a deep sleep.

CHAPTER 22

Sandy was dressed and ready to go by the time Mike was awake.

'There's my wife again. I liked the jeans and leather but you're a classy bird at heart. I love your hair in those knots you do. And the sophisticated suits.' He kissed Sandy on the cheek. 'Remind me of today's agenda?'

'Times Square, although we've missed the walking tour for that. We could do our own tour round it, though, and still have time to get to The Empire State Building for noon?'

'Shame about the tour but I did need the sleep. I'll get ready and we can head off.' Mike went into the bathroom then popped his head round the door. 'And lunch at the Empire Diner on 23rd – that's in Chelsea, I looked it up.'

'Yeah.'

'You see, I do remember the schedule. I'll be ready for a good meal by the time we get there.'

Once on the street they set off at a fair pace. 'Do you fancy going to see the Flatiron Building after the Empire State instead? We could find somewhere to eat on the way.'

'What's the Flatiron Building?'

'It's a huge triangular building – amazing architecture.'

'Nah, too much like work and we might not find a good place for food. It can be such a bore traipsing around finding the best restaurant. Let's stick to the schedule, eh? You've got a booking.' He linked in with Sandy. He was still on a high from his late notice trip and excited to be there.

They arrived at Times Square and meandered around, Mike underwhelmed with it, Sandy unable to dredge up any enthusiasm for sightseeing.

'I guess it's a square we've seen a million times on TV, isn't it? At least it can be ticked off the list.' He bought a pair of Big Apple boxers from a gift kiosk. 'I like travelling light, but a man needs clean pants.'

They stopped at a café on the edge of the square and Sandy sipped her coffee gratefully, hoping the caffeine would liven her up. Mike patted his jacket. 'Passport, tickets, money, pants and toothbrush; everything a man needs.' He took the paperwork out and rifled through it. 'My passport runs out soon. Another ten years have disappeared. I'll need to get a new photo.' He held up the page to Sandy. 'Handsome bugger, don't you think?'

Sandy smiled and agreed.

'I can't remember your picture. Let's see it. Yours'll need renewed at the same time.'

Sandy's stomach somersaulted. Jake still had her passport. Jonjo had handed them to him on Thursday night and she remembered he'd put them in his inside pocket when he took his jacket off for the haircut. She'd forgotten all about it.

'Sandy?'

'I don't have it with me.' Her mind raced. 'It's in the hotel room.'

'In the safe? Good girl.'

The night before she'd been glad she didn't have Jake's number but now it made her panic. How was she going to contact him? Even if he was on the flight back she might not even see him at the airport if he was travelling first class. Would he try to find her if he noticed he still had both?

'Sandy?'

Startled she turned towards Mike.

'Where were you? I've been talking to you.'

'Sorry, I was in a dream.'

'Better snap out of it, we need to get our skates on if we're to get to the Empire State Building by midday.'

They paid the bill and left, Sandy's brain working overtime as she imagined the implications of not having a passport and having to find Jake.

Stepping out of the lift and onto the viewing platform, the panorama blew her worries away. It was a clear day and she could see for miles. Manhattan stretched out before her, and somewhere was Jake. Sandy recalled one of her favourite films – *An Affair To Remember.* If she and Jake were in a movie he would dash onto the viewing platform, brandishing her passport, and they would declare undying love for each other. She searched the crowd of tourists. He was nowhere to be seen of course, only Mike, beside her as always.

'What a view! No wonder there's so many proposals here.' He took her hand. 'Sandy, I have a proposal for you.' She tried to guess what was coming. 'A happy anniversary proposal. It's why I came.' He must be handing in his notice, ready to take a year off.

'The company has offered me a promotion.'

'On this job?'

'No. It's—'

'Mike. You promised this was the last one.'

'Hear me out, Sandy. It's international site director. I would oversee the various company sites throughout the world. It's a huge promotion with almost double the salary and you can travel with me, of course. It includes Brazil, Hong Kong, Beijing, even New Zealand. Ten or twelve places.'

The wind had been knocked out of her sails; she hadn't expected this. 'How long would it be for?'

'It's permanent, sweetheart. Don't you see, this way we can travel, see the world and get paid for doing it.'

Sandy took her hand away. 'What would I do while you're working?'

'I'll have days off.' He smiled encouragingly. 'You'll make friends.'

'But I've decided I want to retrain, go to university, take a course.'

His smile turned to a frown. 'You've never mentioned studying before.'

'These few days have given me a chance to think about the future.'

'You could take courses online, couldn't you? At the same time you could have an adventure and travel the world.' He drew her into him. 'It would be a fresh start for us. We need it. An opportunity like this would do us both good, adventures we could share. We get the best of both worlds. I can still work and we can travel.' He kissed her cheek. 'I love you, Sandy. It was so good to talk last night. Such a weight off – and this offer – I can't believe it. It's ideal for us! They want me in London next week for five days, and straight out from there to Brazil. You could sort things out at the house, pack all our things, and we could be off next week!'

Sandy leaned her head on Mike's chest. It could be the clean slate they needed. Now they had opened up to each other, life might be easier. No more guilt. Less mechanical sex. And lots of people studied online. As Mike embraced her tightly, she tried to conjure up an image of this alternative future. At least they'd be moving away, living an unconventional kind of life.

'Say yes, Sandy, please. It's the best thing for us, and you've always wanted to travel.'

She was strangely numb inside, could see how much he wanted it, how by coming to New York, he was trying. How could she refuse?

'OK. Yes,' she said.

He whirled her around. 'Things'll get much better, you'll see – another future in front of us.'

She smiled and hugged him. 'An adventure.' But somewhere deep inside, her heart was sinking and she closed her eyes tight.

They took the lift down and she checked the time. They'd only spent ten minutes and had hardly appreciated the view. It was ridiculous to think Jake was going to arrive and what would he do anyway? Give her the passport in front of Mike? Madness.

'Let's walk to the restaurant,' she said. 'I could do with the exercise and fresh air.'

Mike checked his watch and searched Google Maps. 'Yeah, you're right, only thirty-four minutes.' He linked her arm. 'You OK?'

She patted his hand. 'I'm fine. It's a lot to take in...my mind's working overtime.'

'That's the spirit, Mrs Stuart. Already planning. Love it.'

CHAPTER 23

Dullard. Imbecile. Chowderhead. He'd always liked chowderhead – mid nineteenth century – stupid or thick-headed person. Origin jolterhead. He'd even waited for her at the side door. Lamebrain.

Jake massaged his forehead, the ache behind his eyes testament to the copious amount of whisky he'd had last night with the guys. Mostly, it had been good fun, being with the band, remembering the past. Inside he couldn't stop thinking about Cassandra Blue. At least he'd got a composition out of it. It was a good song, the best he'd written in years.

Mooncalf – foolish; a simpleton – mid 1500s. So many insults had their roots in the sixteenth and seventeenth century. Why would that be? He must apply himself to research on the subject when he got home. Home to his lair, no-one bothering him. Who was that guy anyway?

Women.

And Zaraya's arrival yesterday for the rehearsal. It was fine. Of course, it was all fine. It was good to see her but she no longer meant anything to him, not in the same way. The jealousy, anger – and love – had gone. He cared about her, was glad she was there and was able to listen to her voice, appreciating the beauty, the skill in how she used it. He'd wished her well with her career, genuinely pleased at her success. They'd all sat around in the bar for hours afterwards, falling about joking, retelling stories from the old days. Oh yes, shaking hands, hugging, kissing and being civil. Before she left Zaraya had mentioned she had a proposition for him, something about a film. He was too drunk to listen, necking the whisky, eating not one but two massive burgers to try and soak the alcohol away. Thank fuck he hadn't thrown the kilt in the bin.

Dingleberry – a foolish or inept person. Only from the 1950s, still a goodie though because here he was being a complete dingleberry atop the Empire State Building at 11.55 am and waiting for ... who, he wasn't sure. In the end, it had been Sandy Stuart who'd waltzed in, with the guy from the night before. There she was, suit on, hideous shoes and those luscious locks pinned away. That had to be her husband. Why had she never mentioned a husband? Only the *I do what I like, when I like, I'm free*' garbage. Another liar. He spied round the corner at them, prepared to duck if Sandy turned in his direction.

At one point he thought he was witnessing a proposal, although the man was wearing a wedding band. He hadn't noticed her wearing a wedding ring. He had looked. She'd removed her hand from the man's at one point, and a discussion had taken place. Of the multitude of skills he'd contemplated learning when he'd been home alone for years, he hadn't considered lip-reading – look how handy that talent would have been.

She'd been in his arms. Lovey dovey with the husy-bandy. It doesn't take much with women does it? Another clodpole about to bite the dust. There's no way she's told him the truth about this weekend. He hoped they'd be eternally unhappy together. Although the way she squeezed her eyes shut when they hugged made him suspect that whatever it was they'd been talking about, it hadn't made her truly happy.

He dived out of the way as they left the viewing platform. They'd barely glanced out at the city, ignored the panorama they'd paid for. He'd also paid for, like a drongo. He still had her passport, found in his pocket when he'd woken with another crashing hangover. The sooner he was safe in his cave, the better. He was tempted to send her passport flying across the city. Rip the pages out and float them into the wind. But that was mean and he wasn't mean, not him. He was a boofhead, a gowk and a dumbass. That's what he was.

CHAPTER 24

Sandy walked beside Mike towards their lunch venue. She was oblivious to the city and the sounds and the smells. Her mind was full of the plan to live abroad and how she could get her passport from Jake. She gave appropriate responses to her husband when his conversation needed it and only came to the present when she recognised the street they were on. The gallery with the Maya Bharoo exhibition was close by.

'Do you mind if we make a detour? There's an exhibition I'd like to see. It's not far.'

'Have we got enough time?'

'I'd allowed an hour for the Empire State Building and we only took ten minutes. Plenty of time.' Sandy led him towards the art in the window.

'Who is it?'

'A woman called Maya Bharoo.'

Mike stared at the display. 'Do you like this? It's a bit of a mishmash isn't it? Let's go to lunch.'

'I'd like to see it. If you don't want to come in, why don't you go and have a drink, over there?'

'Should I get you something too?' Mike sounded unsure.

'No, I won't be long.' She left him and went inside. She spent time with the pieces, finding them remarkable, work she would be able to return to time and again and always gain a fresh insight. They varied in price from hundreds to thousands of dollars.

She came upon a small work, more vibrant in colour than the others, tiny cutouts of lips and eyes and ears, interlocked with each other and, depending how close you were, the tiniest scraps depicted various faces, melding into one. She instantly fell in love with it, the tiny size part of its charm.

The gallerist joined her at the picture. 'This piece is interesting because it's a diptych and comes apart. So you could display it together or separately.' She had to have it, despite the high price tag, and crunched her credit card at the desk while an assistant packaged it up. Sandy slipped it into her backpack.

'If you're a Maya Bharoo fan, don't miss the last viewing room where there's a short video interview from the opening. Keep walking through and you'll find it.'

She moved through the rooms she'd already seen and took her time in the ones she hadn't. Eventually, she could hear talking and she continued on to the video interview with Maya Bharoo herself.

'It was during this dark period I found collage,' Maya was saying. 'Initially, it was a destructive mania; I wanted to cut and slash and couldn't stop. Then I saw how, out of the destruction, I could create fresh pictures and textures.'

'How long did it take you to find your style?' an unseen interviewer asked.

'It was a long time. A long, long time. It was two years before I could leave the flat and it was in a terrible condition, buildings of paper, books and magazines everywhere. My poor partner at the time had to live with it, too. One day I did manage to leave for a couple of hours and when I entered the flat again I saw the disarray with fresh eyes. I saw ways I could bring coherence and another way of working.'

'Did you resume your studies at art college?'

'No, I couldn't face it, I spent time in counselling and I learned I'd been trying to please others by working in a way I believed would make them happy. My parents, my teachers. I was imposing on them the work I thought they wanted to see, wanted me to create. In trying to control my creativity, I was controlling them. Because the truth is we can't make others happy; they must find their own truth to set them free and when I asked myself what I wanted, I set us free. From that point on I got better, no more episodes.'

'Will you be working on a new collection moving forward?'

'I have an international...'

Sandy was no longer listening; the artist's words had resonated so strongly. She was so deep in thought that when the words came round again, the video on a loop for visitors, she listened to it a second time, and a third.

In a daze, she stared unseeing out of a corridor window at a cluttered network of fire exit steps, seeing nothing. Knowledge and revelation tumbled into her head. Mike had never wanted to leave his job at this stage in his career. She was the one who hadn't listened. She had wanted change and she'd pre-empted it by leaving a job she no longer enjoyed. With the agonising years of IVF and the devastating death of Carys, romantic love between them had been lost and now Sandy understood they were never going to find it in a gap year, or while travelling with Mike's job.

In her heart of hearts, as much as her husband would say otherwise, she knew he would be absolutely fine without her. She needed to be her own woman, live a life she wanted and not expect Mike to deny his career for her. She'd been asking him to walk away from his own goals, but he loved his job as much as she had grown to hate hers. She cared about him, but it had been a long time since she'd been in love with him. She wanted to cut the safety net and be Cassandra Blue again, be herself. She stared into the space, thinking about her life.

'Sandy! I thought you'd gone AWOL, you've been so long. You're not even seeing the exhibition.'

She was shocked to see Mike standing there, breaking into her solitude. 'I'm sorry, I—'

'We'll be late if we don't go now.' He took her hand and led her out of the gallery, using his phone to guide them to the restaurant. 'This looks promising, doesn't it?' he said when they arrived outside.

'Yeah, yes, it does.'

He opened the door and they were ushered to their table.

'The burger here is rated one of the best in NYC. Did you know that? I went online to see what they had and I'm going for that. They have a Crispy Chicken Sandwich you'd like. Fancy that? You must be hungry too.'

'I think I am.' She held the menu, the choices a blur before her eyes.

A waiter joined them at the table, pouring water into their glasses. 'And how can I help you good people today?'

'Sandy?'

'I'll have the Crispy Chicken.'

'Fries or salad?'

'Eh, I can't decide.'

'Salad?' Mike asked.

She nodded. Mike added his own burger and two beers and the waiter moved off. 'Is everything alright?'

'Yes, it's fine.' She regarded her husband for a few moments. 'Mike. I have to tell you—'

He shook his head and raised a flat palm towards her. 'Don't, Sandy. Don't say it.'

She went to take his hand but he withdrew from her. 'I'm not going to join you in Brazil' she said. 'I'm sorry. It was a mistake to ask you to leave your job. It's me who needs to change, to find another way of living my life.'

'You can find another way in Brazil. And not only Brazil – there's the other places too. This is our dream – travel, adventure.'

'But you know, it's not really the kind of travelling I meant. It's a compromise and we always compromise these days. As much as you want to go, I want to follow my own path, too.' The tears Sandy had been holding in spilled over.

Mike looked confused. 'Where is this coming from?'

'This weekend, it's been...' She paused to wipe her eyes. 'It's given me space. I've been feeling numb inside for such a long time and this weekend, I've come alive. I have hope. I want to do something with my life.'

'Travelling will be something!' he pleaded.

'Your job means so much to you, and although I shouldn't have asked you to give it up, I don't want to give this up either.'

'I don't understand what "this" is?'

She shook her head, knowing she couldn't make him understand. 'It's the hope that life can be different for me, that I can move on from the past. Find my own freedom.'

'Please come with me, Sandy.' He reached for her and this time she withdrew.

'No.' She took a deep breath and with a courage she didn't know she had, she said, 'I wish you all the love in the world, Mike, but it's the end of the road for us and if you're honest with yourself, you'll know that.'

'We went through so much together; can't we at least try?' He reached out to hold her arm. 'I still love you, sweetheart.'

'And I love you. I also know you wouldn't give up this job for me, would you?' She shook her head at Mike's aghast expression. 'I'm not asking you to, but the job is what you would choose. Can't you see, we no longer want the same things? Perhaps we went through too much together. Too many years of trying, too much heartache and disappointment.'

The waiter arrived and placed their drinks in front of them. Mike wiped away the condensation from his glass. 'I thought coming here this weekend would help – help us find our way back to each other.'

'You see? You feel it too. We love each other, but we're not in love. Not anymore. And don't we each deserve a fresh start?'

Mike took her hand and she held his tightly. The waiter placed their food on the table and they sat, looking in each other's eyes, oblivious to the busy restaurant around them. Minutes passed and they were still sitting holding hands, lost in their individual thoughts.

'Everything OK with your meals?' the waiter asked.

'Everything's fine,' Mike said and he smiled ruefully at Sandy. 'At least we tried.'

'We did. For a long time.'

They sat there, as the food got cold and the beer went flat, contemplating their marriage, and Carys, and everything else that had brought them to this point.

CHAPTER 25

The taxi arrived at the City Hotel and Sandy opened the door. 'You will be careful in Brazil, won't you?' It had amazed her, and Mike, that they'd been able to have an amicable conversation about the future: the dreams he had for his job, how he would find living in Brazil, the architects he'd be working with.

'What are you going to do, Sandy?'

'I'm not sure exactly what yet. Maybe study. It's enough I have the possibility of a new beginning.'

'I'll miss you. I'll keep in touch, and of course, there's our stuff to sort out.'

They hugged each other. 'I'll miss you too,' she said. 'Have a good flight.' She got out and watched the cab drive away, hardly believing the turn of events. She'd split from Mike and she was fine, they would both be fine.

She also had other things to focus on. She strode into the busy hotel reception area and went straight to the lift, a plan already forming. Jake was going to Etta tonight at 6 pm to complete his tattoo. She thought he'd keep the appointment as he'd mentioned it after their shower, both checking their tattoos were still dry and clean. And if he didn't? Beside not having his number, she didn't even know the hotel he was staying at. What had they spoken about when they were together? They'd spoken of music and travel, their childhoods, memories of their home city, their hopes and dreams – nothing practical. If he wasn't there tonight, she would phone the venue and the rehearsal hall, and then all the hotels in Manhattan if she had to. The last resort would be missing the flight and going to the embassy tomorrow morning. But she wanted to see Jake, wanted to explain. Explain about Mike and how she had had no idea he would join her and she hadn't mean to deceive him.

Would he care, though? She remembered he'd said this was just one weekend amongst the hundreds of other weekends they would have in life. And Zaraya had been there last night, sprinkled with the fairy dust that true stars attract. Would it mean something to Jake after ten years of mourning to have her in his life again?

She changed her clothes, now much more comfortable in casualwear than suits. She'd get her passport. They would say goodbye sensibly, and she'd be ready for another chapter in her life. She walked past reception, heading for the revolving doors.

'Mrs Stuart!' The desk attendant waved her over. 'A man dropped something off for you.' She opened a drawer and took out an envelope. 'Here you go.'

Sandy ripped it open. Her passport. 'Did he leave a message?'

'No, he only wanted to leave it for you. Said it was important.'

'Was it a courier?'

'Big guy, greyish hair.' The receptionist smiled. 'Handsome.'

Sandy's stomach sank.

'Are you OK, ma'am?'

Sandy gave a weak smile. 'I'm fine, thanks.' She put the envelope in her backpack and whirled herself out the revolving doors.

Sunday was as busy as any other day; traffic hooted, crowds passed, snatched conversations overheard as she walked. On automatic pilot, she stopped at the road crossings and moved with the flow of pedestrians as she continued down Fifth Avenue. There was no excuse to see Jake, and she felt the gut-wrenching disappointment flooding in with the knowledge she could go on with her life, the romantic interlude over, and never meet him again.

He hadn't even checked whether she was in her room. He obviously had no desire to see her. One foot tripped in front of the other as her mind raced over the last three days, filling her with jumbled emotions. She stopped in the middle of the sidewalk and pedestrians gave loud tuts as they had to move round her. When she became aware of her surroundings, she looked ahead and saw the Flatiron Building. Spotting a café opposite, she went inside, ordered an Americano and sat unseeing as the world went by.

She thought of the passport and realised Jake might have left her a message. She retrieved the envelope and took the passport out, flicking through the pages and shaking the envelope. Nothing. She flicked again. Where were her border stamps from the last ten years? She frowned. This wasn't her passport. She opened it at the photo page and it was Jake who stared at her. He'd left his passport!

She held her hand to her mouth in relief. He'd given her his passport by mistake. She choked a sob and gulped in air at the same time. It was a sign; it must be a sign they should see each other once more. She would take her chances at the tattoo parlour and hope Jake kept the appointment.

It was already 5.30 pm and as soon as she left the café, she tried to hail a taxi. None of them stopped. Yellow cabs, empty and full, sped past, ignoring Sandy's eager hand. Her magic jacket had lost its power. She walked, occasionally giving a hopeful wave, without success. Determinedly she carried on and spotting a subway station, ran down the steps and tapped herself through. The train was busy and it was difficult to hear the guard or see the station signs when they stopped. It was 6 pm by the time she got off, accidentally exiting a stop too soon.

The blue beacon on Google Maps pulsed encouragingly. By now her feet hurt in the boots; they weren't made for this much walking. At last, at 6.40 pm, out of breath, and nervous, she was outside Jonjo's. Through the glass she could see Etta working on Jake's tattoo and she leaned her head against the wall in relief and waited.

Not much time passed before the bell on the shop door gave a loud ting and Jake came out. He stopped when he saw her but then walked on.

'Jake!'

He faced her. 'Why are you here?'

'I'm sorry about Mike arriving. He didn't tell me he was coming.'

'Is Mike your "I can do what I like when I like" husband?'

'Yes. I'm sorry.'

'Everybody's sorry this weekend.'

'I am. Sorry. I would have come to meet you if—'

'You could have told me. Been honest. You don't even wear a wedding ring.'

'I do – on my middle finger. I lost weight when I started running last year and hadn't got it fixed.'

'Bully for you.'

'I didn't not tell you on purpose. This weekend, it's been mad. I've been trying to find something—'

'And you thought it might be me? Ha!'

'No. It wasn't like that. You were the one who said it was just one weekend.'

'Seriously Sandy, you belong to someone else and I don't want to be the person to come between that.'

'You're not, and I don't, I only wanted to—'

'I'm not that kind of guy. Whatever idea you have about me, I'm not that guy. I don't want to be used as a springboard for your marital woes.'

'I'm not using you.'

'Really? It looks to me like that's exactly what you're doing. Out here for a good time without your husband – not exactly faithful behaviour is it?'

'Listen to Mr-Perfect-never-does-anything-wrong-poor-me-Cabrelli! And I've not been unfaithful, I'm leaving my husband. In fact I've left my husband.'

'Didn't look like that to me at the Empire State Building at noon.'

'You were there?'

'Yes. I saw you, being twirled round and hugging each other. Why are you even here?'

'What are you? A stalker? I came for my passport.'

'I dropped it off at the hotel, it's at reception.' Jake turned away.

'Stop!' Sandy thrust the passport at him. 'Open it.'

Jake took it and flicked to the picture page. 'The best laid plans…' he said quietly.

'Give me mine and I'll be on my way.' Sandy wanted to go. The whole situation was leaving a bad taste in her mouth and she wanted to cry.

Jake dug into his inside pocket and got the other passport. He checked inside and handed it over. 'A suitably stuck-up passport picture. I hope the weekend was worth it. You bagged a rock-and-roll man. Was it as good as the teenage fangirl dream? I'm astounded you didn't ask for a selfie to show your groupie friends who you shagged so you could laugh about it afterwards.'

Sandy took a step back, shocked and momentarily speechless as she stared at Jake. 'You egotistical wanker. And you'll know the meaning of that – a contemptibly obnoxious person with a holier-than-thou attitude. Enjoy the rest of your life in solitary confinement. Iain was right: you are an asshole coward!' She turned on her heel and stepped smack into a lamppost.

CHAPTER 26

Jake caught her before she hit the ground. He was a cretin, why did he have such a big cruel mouth? He picked her up easily and took her to Jonjo's, somehow managing to knock on the window while holding her, frightened by the blood coming from her forehead.

Etta opened the door. 'My God. Sandy!' She stood back and Jake angled her body inside as Etta cleared her bag and jacket from the tattoo bed. 'Put her here. How did this happen?'

Jake lifted Sandy onto the bed. 'She walked into a lamp-post. Cassandra. Can you hear me?' He took her hand. 'Cassandra, are you alright?'

'Her name isn't Cassandra, you'll confuse her. Sandy, it's me, Etta.' She took the other hand.

Sandy opened her eyes. 'Ouch, my head hurts,' she said groggily.

'You hit your head on a lamppost. How are you feeling?'

She touched her forehead and her fingers came away slickly wet. 'Blood!'

'It's only a drop. You're used to seeing blood.' He took her hand away and she shook him off.

'Not my blood.' She tried to sit. 'Ugh.'

He helped her lie back. 'Etta, have you got a cloth or something? Some tissue?'

'I've got a first-aid kit.' She ran off.

He gently brushed Sandy's hair away from her face. It was inexplicable why he'd said those things. He was a buffoon. It was all his fault. Clown. Etta brought the kit and he tugged the tissues from her hand, gently wiping blood from the wound. 'Not a serious cut,' he reassured himself.

'Head wounds always bleed a lot,' Etta chimed in.

Sandy opened her eyes.

'Are you dizzy?' he asked.

'No. I'm fine.'

Etta picked up a bottle of antiseptic and poured some on cottonwool.

'I'll do it.' He tussled the wet pad from her hand and cleaned the wound.

'Ow.'

'Don't be a baby. I'll hold it in place for a bit.'

'Get you, Florence.'

'I've got butterfly clips in my first-aid box,' Etta said. 'When the bleeding stops, I'll put them on.'

'Are you still with us?' Jake held the dressing in place.

'It's nipping.'

Etta frowned. 'Nipping?'

'She's sore,' Jake said. 'And Scottish.' He wiped a stray tear trickling across her cheek, while checking the wound for blood flow. 'It's stopped bleeding. Pass me the clips, Etta, and I'll put them on.'

'I'll do it, I know how to do it,' she said.

'It's easier if I do it.'

'Stop fighting you two, or I'll do it myself!'

Jake took the clips from Etta and carefully put them in place. 'How's your head now? Is it sore? How's the cut?'

'Still nipping?' Etta asked helpfully.

'Still nipping.' Sandy smiled. 'Not seeing stars though.'

'Follow my finger,' Jake said.

'Are you a doctor now?'

'Try to be a good patient.' He held his finger in front of his face and Sandy's eyes traced the path back and forth.

'I pronounce you unconcussed.' He helped her sit but she shrugged him off.

'I know I'm unconcussed!' She turned to Etta. 'I'll be fine.'

'You can't go off on your own. She can't be left alone, Jake.'

'I'm fine. I'll get a taxi.'

'Not on your own you won't,' he said.

'Yes, I will.'

Jake sat beside her on the bed, torn between hating her for the hurt she'd caused and wanting to make sure she was OK.

'Sorry guys. I have to go, there's a baby-naming party tonight. Are you sure you're OK, Sandy?'

'Yes. I need fresh air though.' She pushed herself off the bed. 'Thanks, Etta.'

'It's Dr Jake you should be thanking.'

'Happy to be of service,' he said.

Jake found himself ignored as Sandy gave Etta a hug and walked to the door. He could only follow protectively, ready for any relapse. He shouldn't care about her, should still be angry. But he wasn't. And he cared very much.

CHAPTER 27

Outside, Sandy threw off Jake's attempt to take her arm. 'Please don't fuss.'

'I'm not fussing, I want to make sure you're OK.' They walked on in silence.

'I could do with some water,' said Sandy.

'Let's go over there.' They crossed the road to a café and he pulled out a seat for her at an outdoor table. 'Or do you want to be indoors?'

'Outside.'

He went off to the bar. A young hip crowd was full of lively chatter around her. She felt shaky, mostly from the shock of the clang that had reverberated around her head on impact with the lamppost. Jake returned, opened a bottle of water and placed it in front of her.

'Thanks. It's like I'm in a movie again.' Sandy popped out two paracetamol from a pack in her bag.

'Which one?'

'I'm not sure if it's *Diehard* or *Clueless*.'

Jake took a swig of his beer and placed his hands in his pockets. 'I'm sorry. I was being a wanker. I should never have opened my mouth.'

'No, you shouldn't. It wasn't like that at all.' She gently touched her wound and winced. 'This weekend has been utter madness. I have no idea why I didn't say anything about Mike. You were so annoying when we met and it made me angry. I didn't want to be the person you could see I was. And later – this trip – I've been me. Not one of a couple. An individual. And it's been so good. I kidded myself it wouldn't matter, a day or two and we'd never see each other again. I had no idea he was coming. He's never been one for surprises. He called it a grand gesture.'

Jake scraped away at the Bud label. 'Is he still here?'

'No, he left hours ago; he has meetings in London tomorrow.'

'Did he leave after the Empire State Building slot?'

'A little later.' Sandy remembered the silly idea that Jake might come. It transpired he had and while she was persuading herself she could stay with Mike and his job, he had been watching them, and wondering about the kind of woman she was. 'The song. It was breathtaking. Your voice and the lyrics were wonderful.'

'A simple ditty.'

She took a swig of her water with the tablets. 'Why do you say such a thing when it was more than a simple ditty? Did it mean nothing to you? Just another "Cheeky Baby"?'

'Love it or hate it, people always remember cheesy.' Jake hesitated. 'The song was more, of course. It reminded me of the night I found out about Zaraya and Iain. I felt so exposed.' He grimaced. 'There's a lot to be said for being a hermit.'

'I'm sorry. I had no intention of any of this happening. You. My marriage. I've barely seen Isobel because she's been with Chip. When you said something changed for both of us, it did. I won't go home the same person. I've been more alive this weekend than I have in years. I went to the Maya Bharoo exhibition today and it was listening to her interview on a loop that I knew it was me who had to change, to let go. Let Mike go.' She met his gaze. 'I didn't use you, although you've been such a part of this change. And I'm sorry I said those things to you.'

'I deserved it. At least I managed to catch you before you hit the ground – like a dashingly good gallant hero.'

'You think you're a Mr Darcy?'

'I've always seen myself more as a Captain Wentworth.'

'Ooooh. Your Austen knowledge is impressive.'

'Was it a Freudian slip that I left my passport instead of yours at reception?'

'He did say there's no such thing as an accident.'

He held out his hand to her. 'I'm going to show you something even more magical than the leather jacket. C'mon, let's go.'

She took his hand and allowed herself to be led away. They hadn't walked far before Jake whistled loudly. Success.

'Gansevoort Street please, driver.' He got out his mobile. 'I need to text someone.'

'Where are we going?'

'Trust me.' The car sped through the fading light, across the Brooklyn Bridge and Sandy gazed out at the skyline - busy, noisy, and brashly lit - the iconic panorama stretched out before her. So much had happened, it was difficult to take in that it was only a few days ago they'd walked over the bridge and been escorted home by the police. Ordinarily she would have been anxious not knowing where she was going. Instead she was relaxed, unworried. Jake tapped away occasionally beside her.

'How's your head?' he asked.

'Just a dull ache. It's funny, meeting you has been topped and tailed with head injuries.'

'Ouch.' Jake grimaced.

'Whereabouts you going? This is Gansevoort.' The driver asked.

'Here will do.' Jake paid the driver and they walked west. Soon they came to stairs, a sign above read "Highline".

'The Highline – I've heard about this place. Isn't it too dark to walk the track?'

'Patience, woman.'

Sandy followed Jake up the stairs and onto the path, and they walked for about ten minutes - the path lighting where they were going at the same time as revealing Manhattan around them. An old gent appeared, coming slowly towards them.

'Ambrose! Thanks so much for this.'

Jake was pulled into a strong body hug. 'You just caught me in time tonight. It's great to see you, my boy. Where have you been? You fell off the planet.'

'I did, kind of. This is Cassandra.'

'How do, ma'am. C'mon – there's been lots to see tonight, although you're cutting it fine. They'll be closing soon.' They followed him to a large telescope that was trained on the night sky. He moved the dials of the lenses, checked the view and moved aside. 'Here you go, Jake, son. I'm going to store the rest. I'll be back.' He wandered off carrying some equipment.

'An old friend of yours, I take it?'

'When I moved here, there was nowhere to see night skies without driving for miles, and then I read about the Astronomy Club. I used to come as often as I could. Ambrose and Aggie, his wife, became like surrogate parents; even my dad came out to meet them. But I've not been the best at keeping in touch.'

'He's obviously fond of you.'

Jake moved towards the telescope, drawing Sandy with him. 'Put your eye here.' She did as instructed. 'Can you see?'

For a moment there was nothing, and her eye searched around until at the top of the lens she could see Saturn looking glorious in the night sky, the rings clear and defined. It was breathtaking. She looked at Jake and reached out to caress his cheek, not sure she had the words to describe what she was seeing.

'It's moving, isn't it?' he said. 'Ambrose calls it the Saturn Gotcha.'

She looked through the lens again. 'It's extraordinary.'

'Let me show you something else.' Jake moved in and trained the telescope to another part of the sky and guided her back to the lens.

She was conscious of his presence, his body beside hers, so close she didn't want him to move away. She put her eye to the telescope and gasped.

'It's Cassiopeia.'

She was stunned by the clarity. 'I haven't seen anything like it since that night with the school.' She kept looking, blinking away tears, thinking about Carys and stardust and how her daughter was somewhere in the atmosphere and would always be with her. Jake rested a hand on her back and she could feel it, the warmth through the leather jacket onto her skin. She gazed out at the constellation and, as Isobel had predicted, she felt something shift inside; the eternity of space, and the knowledge that Carys was part of the vastness, forever, brought her comfort. The ache of loss would always be part of her but now the love she felt for her daughter surpassed the pain. Sensing her emotion, Jake drew her to him and held her.

Minutes passed as she stood in Jake's embrace until she wiped her tears and he moved behind, encircling her as he repositioned the lens. She brought her eye up close once more and saw the moon, shining brightly. So huge, it filled the lens, the craters of the empty seas clearly visible. She remembered the long-ago night sky she saw, and how Jake found inspiration and creativity in her childish words. She moved aside for him to see, not trusting herself to speak. Instead he looked into her eyes.

'When you look at the stars you're never alone. I've thought about your words so much over the years.' He leaned towards her just as Ambrose arrived flashing a powerful torch. 'What did you see – did it get ya?' he asked Sandy.

'It did. It was magnificent to see it up close like that.'

'Sorry it's so short, Jake, and it's great to see you but I need to get these old bones home to Aggie. My gal worries these days.'

'How's she doing?' Jake expertly packed up the telescope into its case and hoisted it on his shoulder.

'Oh, she's fine and dandy, still misses the postcards you used to send from everywhere. We need to see you proper sometime. Are you here for a while?'

'Leaving tomorrow.'

'Ah, such a shame, you could have come for dinner.' Ambrose led the way and they took another set of steps, back into a street. 'I'll take this from you now. The diner keeps the equipment for us these days which is dandy.'

Jake handed the case over. 'Thanks so much for waiting. I hope you're taking care of yourself, Ambrose.'

'I am, getting old is all.'

'I'm sorry it's a flying visit, that I can't stay longer.'

'No worries, my boy, but don't leave it so long next time. Nice to meet you, Cassandra.' Ambrose disappeared into a nearby restaurant.

'That was such an experience, so moving. Thank you.'

'And thank you for breaking my bad songwriting spell. I think this weekend has been therapeutic for us both. My hotel's near here, we can go there...get something to eat?' As he took her hand she was aware there was another shift between them, a contrast from earlier in the evening. Had he forgiven her for not being honest? Was there hope for them together? Would they see each other in Scotland or was it really just this one weekend? Jake appeared lost in thought too, and when he let go of her hand to let a pedestrian pass between them, she pushed hers into her pockets, not wanting to make any assumptions about tonight. They walked on in a companionable silence through the evening until Jake brought them to a stop on West 23rd.

'You're staying at the Hotel Chelsea?'

'Where else would an old rocker stay?' He opened the door for her and Sandy stepped inside.

CHAPTER 28

'Jake!' Zaraya walked towards them.

'Zaraya. I thought you'd left for LA already.' Jake said.

'I want you to meet someone.' She clasped the elbow of the man next to her. 'This is Leo Coley, the director of *One Hundred Tomorrows*.' The men shook hands.

'Hi,' said Jake. 'Sorry, I've not seen *One Hundred Tomorrows*.' He placed his hand on Sandy's back. 'This is Cassandra—'

Zaraya jumped in. 'Did your agent not tell you about it?'

Jake shook his head. 'I don't always open his emails.'

'It won an Oscar last year and Leo wants you to do the soundtrack of his next film, in Los Angeles.'

'A soundtrack?'

'Yeah, Jake. Do you have time for a drink and I can tell you about it?' Leo asked.

'I'm going home tomorrow.'

'At least hear him out,' said Zaraya. 'It's a brilliant project. The kind of soundtrack you used to speak about.'

Sandy fidgeted and attempted to blend into the background as the conversation flowed around her, leaving her feeling unnoticed and uneasy.

'Are you working on this too?' Jake asked Zaraya.

'Possibly, we've discussed doing a song.' She glanced at the director. 'I suggested you for the soundtrack when I met Leo in LA recently.'

'Jake, I should go.' Sandy went unheard.

'I was already familiar with your songwriting of course, love your work – the breadth of it,' said Leo. 'I didn't know how to contact you but luckily I was introduced to Zaraya; it was such a coincidence that she suggested you too. I'd love you to come to LA so we could work together on the new film.'

'I can't do that.'

'Jake, it's a fantastic opportunity.'

Leo held his hands up. 'One drink. And if you're not interested, I'll go.'

Jake hesitated.

'I'm going to go and leave you to talk about it,' said Sandy, seeing he was undecided.

'Cassandra's right, can't do any harm to talk about it? Let's go to the bar,' Leo said.

Jake turned to Sandy. 'Do you mind? This won't take long.'

'It's better if I go back to my hotel.'

'Come with us. Ten minutes, that's all.'

'OK but I'll wait here, in reception.'

'Are you sure?'

‘Yes.’ She sat in a foyer armchair as they went off into the bar. She could see them through the entrance, sitting close together and Leo talking avidly. He handed Jake a pair of headphones and placed an Ipad in front of him. He watched and listened, joining the conversation with the same animation as the others. Fifteen minutes went by and they were joined by another man – more handshakes and more talking. Sandy could see Jake eagerly paying attention to what was said, then bend to watch the screen again. He pulled off the headphones and his sparkling blue eyes lit up as he spoke and used his hands to emphasise his ideas as the others nodded their agreement. Sandy had no clue what was being said but could see the enthusiasm in his body language as he talked. She was filled with a deep and heavy sadness as she looked on, realising there was no future for them together. His world was not her world and she was mad to have thought it could be. She was a middle-aged fangirl who hadn’t let go of her fantasies.

As she left, the doorman asked if a cab was needed but she refused, deciding to walk, even though it was after 11 pm. For some reason, walking through the centre of the city at this time, on her own, didn’t faze her.

Zaraya. She was stunning and she obviously still wanted to be part of Jake’s life. A life that was so different from Sandy’s - a world of Oscar-winning films, soundtracks and paparazzi.

Her phone rang and Isobel’s image came on screen. ‘Where have you been today?’ asked her friend. ‘You didn’t text me back. Is Mike still here?’

'No, he left this afternoon. I've been to an exhibition and stuff and I'm walking back to the hotel now. How's your day been? I didn't notice your text, sorry.'

'We went to the Empire State after breakfast and then meandered with Chip's guidebook. When should we leave in the morning? It's 6.30 am on the schedule.'

Sandy hesitated. '7 am would be fine, I think. I'll book a taxi.'

'God, this weekend has been something else. We're going to have so much to talk about on the plane, we'll never sleep. Are you on your own?'

'Yes, on my own.'

'Whirlwind romance over then?'

'Let's do our debrief tomorrow. Sleep tight. If you do sleep!'

Isobel snorted. 'Night.'

Sandy ended the call and kept walking.

In the hotel room she packed, a trifle difficult as her wardrobe had expanded over the weekend and no longer fitted the small carry-on. She placed the sensible shoes on one of the chairs and carefully folded the suit, the pussy bow blouse, and anything else neutral she found, on top of it. She vowed there would be no more beige in her life.

She contemplated her future without Mike, then quickly drifted to the thought of never seeing Jake again. Should it be enough that the future was hers and she'd been in Jake's life for this one weekend?

Her mobile pinged. Mike. 'Landed safely. Spent the flight thinking about us, and the good times. Wishing you all my love for your new life.'

She climbed into bed and, for the first time in years, cried herself to sleep.

CHAPTER 29

It was the knocking again, interrupting her dreams. She picked up her phone – 5.30 am. Had she dreamt it? There it was again. A very gentle but insistent tapping. She heard a voice say, 'Cassandra.'

She wrapped the sheet around her and opened the door. 'Jake?'

He brushed past her, buzzing with energy. 'I'm going to LA. Leo is great. It's so exciting, he wants a soundtrack linking to the dialogue and action, in a way no-one's ever done before.' He circled the room as he told Sandy of the meeting. 'I need to be there so I can be involved in the script, shoot and edit, from the get-go. We spoke for hours about it. No whisky! He's full of ideas and he liked mine too. My head's exploding with it.'

'It sounds fabulous. You said you needed something new. And Zaraya?'

'Zaraya? She only wanted to make the introduction. And when Leo met her she knew where I'd be staying for the gig.' Jake stopped. 'Why did you leave? I came to get you to join us but you'd disappeared.'

'I felt out of place. And Zaraya was there. I didn't want to be in the way of anything.'

He looked confused. 'She's not part of my life anymore. I think her trying to do this for me is her way of saying sorry.'

Sandy looked at his face, honest and earnest in the early morning light and knew she believed him. 'Anyway, it does sound a fantastic opportunity; you should take it.'

'I know.' He paced the room, then stopped in front of her, 'Don't go home. Come with me to LA. I'm getting the 9 am flight from Newark.'

'That's crazy. I can't do that.'

'This has been a crazy weekend. Come with me, you can study there; we can make it work. God, it's the Mecca of psychoanalysts! There'll be a million courses.'

'I can't come with you to LA, Jake. It's not my world.'

'How can it not be your world?'

'Music, films, directors, LA. I'm plain ordinary Sandy Stuart.'

'No you're not. You're Cassandra Blue. You said it yourself on the Brooklyn Bridge. You're Cassandra Blue - inspirational woman of the magic jacket who is not afraid of a square go!'

Sandy smiled at the memory of their mad time together.

'Come with me. Let's continue this weekend; let's see where it goes. You can get a study visa.'

'I wish we'd met a long time ago. At one of those school dances you played at.'

'We weren't the same people then, just kids. This is now. It'll be an adventure!'

'I've decided not to go on Mike's adventure. This would be yours. I need to find my own.'

'This can be yours. You'll be free to do anything you like, and I'll help you in every way possible.' He took her hands in his. 'You know there's something special between us. You must feel it too. I think I fell in love with you that night, as a teenager, watching you on TV. Cassandra, we're meant to be together. Come with me.'

They stared at each other. Sandy's heart swelled at his words just as she was gripped by fear of the unknown. Would this be her adventure or Jake's?

'I'm sorry. I can't.' She stepped away from him.

Jake closed his eyes for a moment, his shoulders hunched and defeated. 'I have to go. I have to do this.'

'I know you do. I'm sorry.' She looked into his eyes, then had to look away.

He took a deep breath. 'Goodbye Cassandra Blue.'

She watched him leave.

CHAPTER 30

'Oooh Cassandra! I'm not sure you're going to get an upgrade this time in your leather and jeans.'

Sandy smiled as Isobel fell into a chair in the hotel reception.

'I've left Chip in the room; his flight's not 'til later. Hope he doesn't raid the mini bar, it's still on my credit card.'

'Let's go wait outside for the taxi. A last blast of New York vibe.' They exited the hotel and parked the cases on the sidewalk. Isobel looked at Sandy. 'I've hardly seen you this weekend! You have to tell me what's happening. Is everything alright with Mike? And did you hear anything from Jake?'

Sandy didn't answer immediately. 'He left my hotel room an hour ago.'

'What? You actually saw him again?'

A shiny black sedan appeared and the driver honked. Jonjo jumped out towards them, followed by Etta. 'Hey girl, I'm coming for the ride,' she cried.

Sandy kissed her cheek. 'It's great to see you. And this is my friend, Isobel. Isobel, this is Etta and Jonjo. It was Etta's sister's baby we delivered.'

'Wow. That was some luck you had this midwife hanging round your neighbourhood.'

'You're deadass right, it was.'

Jonjo shook Isobel's hand. 'Pleased to meet ya. Let's get these bags away.' He lifted their luggage into the boot.

'How's your head, Sandy?' Etta asked.

'It's fine, thanks.'

'Your head?' Isobel was confused.

She lifted her hair away and showed off the butterfly clips. 'A long story for the plane. Let's get going.' They settled into the sedan.

'Newark Airport, ma'ams?'

'Yes, please.'

Jonjo put on some of the Juan Luis Guerra he'd played only days before.

'Spill, Sands. What did you tell Mike? Is he suspicious?'

'Mike and I are over. He's got a huge promotion that means he'll be working abroad. He's off to Brazil in a few days.'

Jonjo and Etta exchanged glances as they earwigged the conversation.

'Sandy! You've only known Jake for a couple of days. Are you going to let a little fling ruin twenty years of marriage? This is real life. You and Mike are made for each other.'

'At one time, not anymore.'

'You don't know how lucky you are.'

Now Sandy was impatient. 'I do, Isobel. I do. But Mike and I ... things between us have not been good for a long time and I can't stay in the same place just because you want me to!'

Isobel was quiet for a while, then said, 'I only want the best for you.'

'Then be my friend and support me. Don't make me feel bad for wanting something different.'

'Wow. Some weekend for you. I still think you're mad.'

'I'm the sanest I've been in years. And it's nothing to do with Jake. It's me. I shouldn't have been asking Mike to throw away a career he loves, when I was the one who needed to move on and change my life. This isn't about you and Brian; this is about *my* life.' She spoke more harshly than she intended, and they stared out of their respective windows for a while.

Jonjo and Etta raised eyebrows at each other in the front. The sleek sedan purred on to the airport, easing in and out of the busy traffic. Sandy watched the buildings as they whipped by, thinking of how she and Jake had sped numerous times across the city, the constant movement adding to the confusion she felt about everything that had transpired. The car dipped into the Lincoln Tunnel and she was mesmerised by the flashing lights and traffic streaming past until they came into the bright sunshine again.

Eventually Isobel squeezed Sandy's hand. 'I'm sorry Sandy, you're right. I've held on to your marriage to Mike. It comforted me in a way to imagine Brian and I would have been together always if things had been different. I couldn't hear you when you spoke about your unhappiness. Maybe Brian and I wouldn't have stayed together and I might have been out there on the dating apps anyway.'

'I'm sorry too. And I do understand. But it's good you're moving on. It might not be Chip, but there'll be someone out there.'

'I hope so. It appears to have been a transformative weekend for both of us.'

'You'll be on Tinder as soon we get home.'

Isobel laughed. 'I already had a peek this morning. Slim pickings, let me tell you. And what about Jake? Is he going to be on the flight to Edinburgh?'

'No. He was, but now he's going to work in LA.'

'But you'll see him again?'

'No.' Her voice cracked as she spoke and she swallowed. 'It's been a rollercoaster.' She bit her lip, suppressing the threatening tears.

'Did he want to see you again?'

A tear rolled down Sandy's cheek. 'He asked me to go to LA with him.'

'Oh my God! What did you say?'

'I can't.'

Etta chimed in from the front seat 'Why not? Jake's a good man.'

'I can't go to LA. My marriage only finished yesterday. I need to consider my future, make a plan.'

Isobel said sharply, 'You've already decided your marriage is over. You slept with the gorgeous Jake Cabrelli – who wrote a song about you and sang it live on stage – and now you need to consider your future?'

'What are you saying? A minute ago you wanted me to stay with Mike.'

'I didn't appreciate how it was between you two. Surely you're leaving Mike because you met Jake?'

'Yeah, watcha doing?' Etta chimed in again. 'You two have got something going on, I could see it on Thursday night – and yesterday. You can't be throwing love away!'

'I can't be part of his life. Who am I going to be in LA?'

'The same person you'd be at home,' Isobel said. 'How do you feel about never seeing him again?'

Sandy couldn't speak, she brushed the hot tears from her face.

'Do you love him?' her friend asked gently.

The car idled in a queue of traffic. 'I think I've fallen in love with him. But it's impossible.'

Etta threw another two cents into the argument. 'I think he's in love with you. I saw the way he looked at you when you were nearly conked out and all.'

'When is he leaving?' Isobel asked.

'An hour before us.' Sandy stared out the window.

Jonjo took the exit for the airport and they arrived at Departures. They got out and he offloaded everything to the sidewalk.

'Sandy, I forgot to show you something.' Etta skimmed through her phone. 'Here's the little baba.' On the screen was a photo of the baby girl Sandy had delivered. 'And guess what they're going to call her? Carys. Doesn't it suit her? An adorable name for an adorable girl.'

Sandy could hear Isobel's sharp intake of breath and she was stunned too. She took the phone from Etta and zoomed into the tiny face.

'I don't know the Carys you got the tattoo for, but this one's a honey,' said Jonjo.

Isobel gawped at Sandy. 'You got a tattoo?'

'She did. And because you met Mr Crazy Kilted Man on the plane, a bit of Carys will forever be in New York.' Etta held up her phone with the picture as evidence.

Isobel placed herself in front of her friend. 'Sandy, do you remember what you said to me on the flight out?' "You have to take every opportunity in life because you can't see the future." Your words.'

Sandy's heart was thumping. 'What do I do?'

Isobel gripped her shoulders. 'You go and get Jake Cabrelli.'

'You'll want Terminal A.' said Jonjo. 'Happy to drive, although you'll be much quicker on the AirTrain.'

'You have to go. Right now.'

Sandy hugged Isobel. 'Thank you, thank you so much, dear friend.' She hugged Etta and Jonjo. 'And thank you both, for everything. Isobel, could you get Carys sent to my phone?' She grabbed the handle of her case, ready to run. 'And can you pay Jonjo?'

'This one's on us! Go, go!'

CHAPTER 31

Sandy ran through the automatic doors and checked the departures board. Jonjo was right. There was a LA flight from Terminal A at 9 am. The airport was teeming with people as she fought her way through to the AirTrain and jumped aboard. They arrived minutes later and she was still none the wiser as to how she was going to find Jake in a sea of people. The best plan was to get through security and find the departure gate. Hoping he hadn't already boarded the flight by the time she got there, she joined the long queue, keeping an eye out for any sign of him. He was tall; she'd spot him easily. The crowd crept forward at a snail's pace. Twenty minutes later she was at the entry point and placed her mobile ticket on the scanner. It beeped loudly and glowed red. She tried again only to be met with the same resistance. She checked it was the right ticket on the app. Yes. She tried again. Beep. Red.

'Can I help you, ma'am?'

'Yes. I'm trying to get through and for some reason it won't let me.'

'Let's see your ticket.' She showed it to her.

'You're in the wrong terminal, ma'am. This is for internal flights. You're going to Edinborrow.'

Sandy could hear tuts and mutters behind her. 'I know, but I want to get through to find someone. It's important, can't I go through?

'No, you can't, lady. You have to go to Terminal C.'

'Please, I may never see him again and—'

'The only way you can get through here is if you have a valid ticket. Please step aside and let these nice folks move on to their destinations.' The attendant ushered her out of the way.

She crushed back through the queue, still trying to spot Jake. Of course she would need a ticket, why was she wasting time? Sandy ran along the concourse. Arrows showed the direction to the sales desk and she ran on, bumping her carry-on behind her. Frazzled, she joined a smaller queue, edging forward even more slowly than the earlier one. Sandy played with fate – if she couldn't get a ticket it wasn't meant to be, although she gave an involuntary whimper at the thought.

It was madness – had he been serious about wanting her to come to LA? Had he asked her because he felt obliged to, because he was scared of going on his own? Could he want her? She cast her mind to their time together, trying to read any other sign into his invitation. She waited impatiently; passengers must be boarding by now.

At last she was called forward and as she wheeled her case, her backpack fell off the top and its contents splayed across the floor, the schedule disappearing under the counter. She scrabbled the rest together and moved forward to the desk, hands full of her possessions.

'I'd like a ticket to Los Angeles, please, on the 9 am flight.'

'I'm not sure if you'll make it, let me see if there are any seats.'

'I don't mind where I sit. I only need one seat.'

The saleswoman tapped away on the keys, a bored expression on her face. 'The 9 am is full. I can get you on the 13.45?'

'It has to be the 9 am. Is there nothing at all?'

'There may be something.' Interminable minutes went by. 'We have one seat in business class.'

'I'll take it.' Still clutching her belongings, she tipped them into her bag, dropping bits and pieces on the way.

'I don't know if you'll be able to get through security and to the gate in time. Do you want me to see if there's anything available on the 13.45?'

'I'll make it, please just give me the ticket.' Sandy scrabbled for her wallet, emptying the contents again to find it – the diptych, liquids bag, passport, her phone.

'It's currently a twenty-eight-minute wait for departures' security and it's thirty-two minutes until the flight closes. That's $1270 please.' The attendant pushed the card reader towards her.

'Give me two seconds.'

The next traveller came towards the desk as Sandy continued the search for her wallet.

'Ma'am do you want to step aside while you find it?' asked the attendant.

'It's here, I've got it.' She waved it about, jubilant. 'It was in my jacket!' The ticket was issued and Sandy scooped her belongings together.

'You will have to hurry, ma'am; and the ticket is non-refundable.'

Sandy ran but was stopped abruptly by the long queue to get through security. She hopped from one foot to the other, bursting with frustration as the horde of people in front of her remained static. Minutes ticked by. This was impossible.

She suddenly raised a hand in the air. 'Midwife coming through. Please make way,' she yelled. 'Baby being born on the other side.' The bemused crowd parted creating a path for her as she kept shouting. 'Midwife coming through. Someone's giving birth. I'm needed.'

Reaching the entry point at the top of the queue, she slammed the ticket on the scanner and it gloriously beeped her through. She sailed through security in only a few minutes and searched the information for the gate number. Gate 32, eleven minutes' walk according to the sign. And six minutes until boarding closed. Jumping on the travelator, she squeezed passed luggage and passengers, ticket and passport in hand. She ran on until she eventually arrived at the gate, incapable of speech, and showed her documents to the attendant who waved her through.

Hands shaking and legs trembling with the effort, the steward directed her to a seat in business class. As she moved through the small cabin, there was no sign of Jake. She searched the aisles. He wasn't there.

'Could you take your seat please, ma'am, and fasten your seat belt.'

Sandy took her seat and buckled up. Every so often she would look around but there was no sign of him boarding. A seat adjacent to her was unoccupied, perhaps it was Jake's and he'd changed his mind. She was an idiot. He wasn't even on the flight. And she was on her way to LA – alone. Why had she been so scared? She was a fool and a coward. A nincompoop! This was a ridiculous idea. She undid her belt and stepped into the aisle.

There was Jake.

'Cassandra!'

Seeing him in front of her, she was barely able to ask the question, 'Did you mean what you said about LA?'

A passenger squeezed past as she waited for his answer. Holding her breath.

'More than anything.' He stood before her - not the teenager she first had a crush on, and not the broken recluse she'd met only days before – but the man she wanted to share her new life with.

'I've fallen in love with you, only I was too scared to admit it.' She looked into his eyes, her heart thudding in her chest as he took her in his arms, oblivious to the packed cabin looking on, and his lips found hers.

When they broke apart, he kept her close and whispered, 'And I am completely canged by you.' Sandy leaned away and regarded him with a raised brow.

'It's from the Middle English period meaning besotted and mesmerised.'

'Moving away from the study of insults then?'

'It's only going to be the language of love from now on.' They smiled at each other then laughed self-consciously as they became aware of a ripple of applause from their fellow travellers.

'Please, you must take your seats.' A stewardess requested, grinning at them both as they did so.

And, as Sandy buckled up and Jake reached to take her hand in his, she knew she was ready for any adventure that lay ahead.

AFTERWORD

I hope you enjoyed Just One Weekend and if you would like others to enjoy it too, then please leave a review – on Amazon, on social media, anywhere you choose – it's so helpful for a new author to find their audience.

Look out for my debut novel The Liberation of Bella McCaa – the trials and tribulations of a fifty-something woman navigating life and love while trying to get her life back on track after ten years as sole carer to her mother. Join my mailing list over at www.catherineaitken.com for up-to-date news.

Thank you so much for reading Just One Weekend.

ACKNOWLEDGEMENTS

Many people helped me get to this stage and I have appreciated all the wonderful support. But there are those who need a special mention - my sisters, Maggie Aitken and Janet Begg have read every draft and happily given feedback - and allowed me to speak about my ideas ad nauseum - thank you for everything. Insightful editing skills and assessments came from editor Sam Boyce and Ellie Hawkes of Elspells Writing Feedback. Friends Alison Craig and Caroline O'Meara need a special mention too, for all the help and support they've given to this book. The beautiful book cover design is by Raspberry Creative Type. And last but not least - to all the friends and colleagues, in Scotland and New York, who commented on and critiqued early drafts, and supported my writing life in all different ways - a huge thank you. I couldn't have done it without you.

Printed in Great Britain
by Amazon

45138567R00128